# Maybe

The curly-haired guy dropped his red backpack on the first row of seats and glanced at one of the adult chaperons. "Yo," he called. "Is this where the Rain Forest amigos are hangin'?"

I couldn't seem to tear my eyes away from him. I guess I must have been staring a little, because he noticed me. And then—he smiled. Needless to say, I was totally embarrassed. I couldn't believe he'd caught me gawking at him. I was about to turn away.

But then for some reason Jessica's voice popped into my head with one of her all-time favorite phrases: "Go for it, Lizzie!"

And suddenly I knew what she would do if she were in my place right now. If Jess had been staring at a cute guy and he'd caught her, she wouldn't just blush and turn away. No, she'd do something bold and daring, like wink at him or blow him a kiss. That made me wonder if maybe I hadn't been too shy around guys in the past. Maybe now that I was almost in eighth grade I needed to start being more daring, like Jessica. What harm could it do to try it out and see what happened?

All these thoughts raced through my head in about half a second. So the curly-haired guy was still smiling at me when I decided to follow my twin's advice and go for it. I'm not as bold as Jessica is, so I couldn't quite bring myself to wink or blow kisses. I decided to start simple: I smiled back.

Visit the Official *Sweet Valley* Web Site on the Internet at:

**http://www.sweetvalley.com**

SWEET VALLEY TWINS

# Elizabeth: Next Stop, Jr. High

Written by
Jamie Suzanne

Created by
FRANCINE PASCAL

BANTAM BOOKS
NEW YORK·TORONTO·LONDON·SYDNEY·AUCKLAND

RL 4, 008-012

ELIZABETH: NEXT STOP, JR. HIGH
*A Bantam Book / November 1998*

*Sweet Valley High® and Sweet Valley Twins® are
registered trademarks of Francine Pascal.*

*Conceived by Francine Pascal.*

*Produced by 17th Street Productions,
a division of Daniel Weiss Associates, Inc.
33 West 17th Street
New York, NY 10011.*

*Photography by Michael Segal*

ISBN: 0-553-49237-3

*Published simultaneously in the United States and Canada*

Bantam Books are published by Bantam Books, a division of Bantam
Doubleday Dell Publishing Group, Inc. Its trademark, consisting of the
words "Bantam Books" and the portrayal of a rooster, is Registered in the
U.S. Patent and Trademark Office and in other countries. Marca
Registrada. Bantam Books, 1540 Broadway, New York, New York 10036.

PRINTED IN THE UNITED STATES OF AMERICA

OPM    0 9 8 7 6 5 4 3 2

*To Mia Sanitsky*

# One

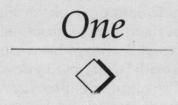

Dear Diary,

Well, here I am on my way to the airport. I can hardly believe the big day is finally here! I'm excited but kind of nervous too. This isn't the sort of thing I expected to be doing the summer before eighth grade. Of course, eighth grade may not be anything like what I was expecting either, so I guess it all kind of makes sense.

Jessica is sleeping next to me in the backseat. Actually, to be completely accurate, she's sleeping *on* me and drooling on my shoulder. I'm a little surprised she decided to come along and see me off—we all know how she feels about her beauty sleep, and it *is* pretty early.

I'm glad she came, though. It's going to be

incredibly strange being apart from her for such a huge chunk of the summer. Five weeks is a long time. Especially since Jessica and I have never really been separated before, not for more than a few days. Even though there are moments—OK, sometimes whole days or weeks or months—when I think that Jess and I have absolutely nothing in common, we've still always been close. They say that's how it is with twins, and I guess it's true.

In a way, this summer is proof of how different we are. Because if Jessica and I were exactly alike (like some people think when they see our identical long blond hair and blue-green eyes), we would both be spending the month of August in the same place. Instead I'm off to Costa Rica while Jessica is staying behind in Sweet Valley to hang with her friends in the Unicorn Club.

Jessica isn't the only one I'm going to miss. There's Mom and Dad, of course, and Steven (even though he'd never admit it, I know he'll miss me too). I'll definitely miss my friends, especially Maria Slater—she's the one who gave me this travel diary as a going-away present. She said she picked it out because it's small enough to take with me everywhere. She's smart that way.

"See? It's smaller than those paperback mystery novels you're always carrying around," she told me when I unwrapped it.

"Thanks, Maria," I exclaimed, running my fingers over the cloth-covered diary. "It's perfect!"

"You'll probably be too busy to read much on this trip. But you ought to write down everything that happens so you'll always remember it." She smiled. "Of course, the way you write, it will probably turn out sounding like a novel anyway."

"Thanks," I said again, reaching over to give her a hug. Leave it to a good friend like Maria to know me so well—and to choose the perfect gift! She really understands how important this trip is to me. In fact, I liked the diary idea so much, I bought one for Jess and left it on her pillow. She'll have a little surprise waiting for her when she gets back from leaving me at the airport!

I still remember how excited I was when I first found out about the Rain Forest Friends and their work. It was a few weeks after school let out for the summer. I was browsing the Internet for information I could use in an article I was writing for the school newspaper. The article was about student volunteering, and I was finding tons of interesting stuff I could use.

After a while I came across a link that mentioned California teen volunteers. That's when I found it—a Web site about an organization called Rain Forest Friends that sponsors teenagers to go all over Central America to help with lots of different projects. They had an urgent notice on the site, asking for volunteers ages twelve and up from southern California to join a trip to an area of Costa Rica that recently suffered heavy flood damage.

The villagers in the area had lost a lot of buildings—houses, community centers, schools—that they needed help rebuilding.

"Wow," I whispered, staring at the computer screen. It was almost *too* perfect—I mean, I'm thirteen years old, I live in Sweet Valley, California, and I've even done some volunteer work with Houses for Humans, so I have a little bit of experience with building. Plus I've always believed that volunteering is really important. I've spent a lot of time working at the local homeless shelter and other places, and it always makes me feel great to help someone else. The Costa Rica project sounded like an incredible way to spend part of the summer. I quickly scanned the rest of the Web site, then took down the phone number and went to talk to my parents.

I found them in the living room, reading the newspaper. They listened carefully as I told them all about the Web site and the Costa Rica project.

"Costa Rica?" my dad said when I finished, wrinkling his brow like he always does when he's thinking hard about something. Mom looked thoughtful too. "That sounds like a very interesting and worthwhile trip, Elizabeth," she said. "But Costa Rica is awfully far away. And you've never traveled that far on your own before."

I could tell what they were thinking—that I was kind of young to be heading off to the rain forests of Central America all alone. I didn't blame them for being nervous. That's their job as parents. But I had to make them understand that I could handle it.

"I know," I said. "But I wouldn't be by myself, not really. I'd be with a whole group of kids from nearby towns plus some adult supervisors."

Dad was nodding. "True," he said. He exchanged a glance with my mother. "Give us a little time to think it over, Elizabeth. Oh, and let me have that phone number so I can call the Rain Forest Friends and check them out."

I gave him the piece of paper. "Thanks," I said. "Whatever you two decide, I want you to know I appreciate that you're considering it."

Mom smiled and patted me on the arm. "You're welcome. Now could you set the table for dinner, please?"

"Sure, Mom." I headed toward the kitchen, humming under my breath. From the way my parents looked and sounded, I was feeling optimistic that they would say yes. *Costa Rica, here I come!* I thought happily.

Jessica thought I was nuts, of course.

I guess she overheard my parents talking about it because the first thing I knew, she was storming into the kitchen with her hands on her hips. "Are you crazy, Elizabeth?" she cried. "Why would you want to go to some lame rain forest where there isn't even any decent shopping?"

"Come on, Jess." I opened a cabinet and took

out five plates. "It'll be interesting. Besides, I'll be helping people who need it. It's not like I'll be bored."

She rolled her eyes, opened the refrigerator, and grabbed a diet soda. "Yeah, right," she said. "Chopping your way through some snake-infested rain forest for the excitement of doing manual labor? Living in native huts where there probably isn't indoor plumbing or even a place to plug in your hair dryer? That sounds a little *too* interesting to me." She slumped down into her chair and popped the top on her soda.

"It's not going to be like that," I protested. "The villages we'll be helping are really more like towns. There's plumbing and electricity and everything."

"But I thought we were going to spend the whole summer relaxing and getting ready for our big eighth-grade year," Jessica said, pouting. This is probably a good time to mention that our school district is getting rezoned for next year—and nobody knows where they'll be going to school or with whom. I think Jessica has been feeling a little nostalgic and wanting to spend as much time as possible with her friends. She's probably worried that things will never be the same again if the Unicorns get split up. But at least she and I can be certain that *we* won't get split up.

I shoved her soda can aside so I could set down her plate. "There will still be time for that," I reminded her. "The trip to Costa Rica isn't until

August." I sighed. "Besides, I'm not sure I'll want to spend too much time sitting around and thinking about our big eighth-grade year. Not until we know more about what's happening."

Jessica just shrugged and waved her hand at that, as if she wasn't worried at all. But I know she really is, and I am too. That's another good thing about going to Costa Rica—I won't have to spend my summer worrying about whether I'll get sent to a new school or not!

So I was thrilled—even if Jessica wasn't— when my parents decided that I could go to Costa Rica if I really wanted to. They said it was because I've always been so responsible and mature. That made me feel good, even though I think Jessica was sort of annoyed. She always tells me that being responsible and mature are way overrated, but I guess this time she was wrong.

Once I knew I was going, the days seemed to fly by. Maria helped me do more research on the Internet and at the library so I'd be prepared for life in Costa Rica. She even found an old Spanish phrase book in her attic.

Maria and I also found some information on the Net about constructing simple buildings. The most interesting Web site was called "Coco's Cost-Cutting Construction Concepts." I printed out that one since I thought it might come in handy. I know the Rain Forest Friends work with pretty tight budgets, so any cost-cutting tips should be useful.

After all her help, I was hoping that Maria might decide she wanted to come to Costa Rica with me. But she's been accepting more acting jobs lately, and she got hired to star in a made-for-TV movie that would be shooting during July and August. I was sort of disappointed when I realized that I wouldn't know anyone on the trip. Oh, well, I'd just have to make friends.

Still, part of me was glad to be leaving Sweet Valley for a little while. I said something about that to Maria when we got together the other day. "I liked things at Sweet Valley Middle School the way they were," I told her, playing with the ruffle on my pillowcase. "I don't know if I'm ready to have them change."

Maria nodded. "You mean all this talk about the new districting and stuff? We still don't know for sure that it's going to happen."

"But we know that it *probably* will," I reminded her. "I heard some of us may be reassigned to a new junior high school and that we might get mixed in with the kids from Secca Lake. If that's true, eighth grade may not be anything like we were expecting."

"It may be better," Maria said hopefully. "We might get to meet lots of cool new people and get out of our rut."

I shrugged. "I liked our rut. And what if we can't stand the new people?"

Maria looked at me in surprise. "That doesn't sound like you, Elizabeth," she said. "I thought you liked trying new things. Like this trip to Costa Rica, for instance."

I shrugged again. "This is different," I said quietly.

I don't think she understood what I was so worried about. But I was definitely worried. Was I ready to handle all these changes? At SVMS the teachers and classes and activities were familiar. All the other students knew what to expect from me. I knew what to expect from them. And this fall Jess and I and our friends were finally supposed to get to be in charge. I would edit the school paper and maybe the yearbook. Maria would be president of the drama club. Jess and Lila seemed to think they were shoo-ins to be cocaptains of the Boosters, Sweet Valley Middle School's cheerleading squad.

Now we might have to start over. Nothing will be the way we thought it was going to be. We're all going to have to prove ourselves all over again.

Oh, well. I guess whatever is going to happen will happen, and we'll just have to get used to it— somehow. All I can say is that I'm going to concentrate on having a great experience in Costa Rica—so that no matter what happens when eighth grade starts, at least I'll have a wonderful summer adventure to look back on.

Well, Diary, I'm on my way! Our plane took off a little while ago, and we're settled in for the long flight to Costa Rica. It's all starting to feel more real, and that makes me more nervous and excited than ever.

Jessica actually woke up long enough to come inside the airport with the rest of us (even though she totally denied she'd been drooling, even after I showed her the huge wet slobber spot on my T-shirt!). I noticed she'd brought a white plastic shopping bag with her, but when I asked her about it, she stuck it behind her back.

"Not until we get inside," she said, with one of those mysterious eye twinkles that means she's up to something. I figured I'd find out what it was soon enough. Jessica can never keep a secret for long.

I was starting to get choked up as we went through security and walked toward my gate. Mom was holding my hand, and all I could think about was how I wouldn't see her—or any of them—for five whole weeks. It was such a bizarre feeling, I couldn't talk much while we were walking. I didn't really know what to say, and I was afraid if I said any of the stuff I was thinking, I would burst into tears.

Finally we got to the gate and sat down near the front. Almost nobody else was there yet—we were kind of early, which was my fault, I guess. I like to be on time, and I definitely didn't want to miss my plane, so I made sure we left the house way before we needed to. The only other person sitting in our section was a pretty girl with dark hair who had spread her stuff out on the last row of seats, near the candy and soda machines. I later found out that her name is Tanya—she's part of the Rain Forest Friends group too. But I didn't think about her too much at the time because I was too busy trying not to cry.

Mom seemed kind of choked up too because she didn't say much. She just kept telling me to "be careful" and "make sure you take your vitamins." Dad pretty much said the same stuff, though he also added "send us lots of postcards so we know you're doing OK." Steven kept telling them to get a grip.

I guess Jessica finally had enough of their weepy looks because she stood up and grabbed my arm in one hand and that white plastic bag in the other.

"We'll be right back, OK?" she told our parents. "I think Lizzie and I need a moment alone."

I was kind of surprised. Jessica usually isn't the sentimental type. I let her drag me over behind a soda machine where Mom and Dad couldn't see us. The only people around were that dark-haired girl and a small gaggle of girls a little younger than us who were pumping change into the soda machine and talking loudly about how much they'd loved their trip to southern California.

Jessica didn't notice the other kids at all. She was digging around in that plastic bag of hers.

"OK, Lizzie," she said briskly. "I know you, so I'm sure you probably didn't think about how long five weeks really is."

"I'm just starting to realize it," I began, assuming she was feeling the same way I was. "I don't know how I'm going to—"

She interrupted me before I could go on. "That's why I decided it was up to me to make sure you had the necessities for a trip of this kind."

(Actually, looking back over what I just wrote, I'm not sure I got that last quote quite right. Jess doesn't usually use words like *necessities*. She probably said something more like "all the majorly important stuff you'll totally die without.")

Anyway, she went on to pull a bunch of rock CDs and movie magazines out of her bag. She showed them to me, looking very proud of herself.

"See?" she said. "This way you'll have something to do at night after a boring day of hammering and sawing or whatever." She kind of shuddered when she said that, probably imagining how awful my fingernails were going to look by the end of the trip.

"Thanks, Jess." I didn't know what else to say. The materials the Rain Forest Friends sent me after I signed up specifically asked us to leave American pop culture—in other words, stuff like CDs and movie magazines—at home so we'd be able to give the local culture a chance. I planned to follow that advice. I didn't even pack any American books except one mystery novel to read on the plane. I figured I'd be too busy to read once I got to Costa Rica anyway, just like Maria said. And if I did have any spare time, I planned to spend it writing down my daily experiences in this diary.

But I knew Jessica would never understand any of that. And I didn't want to hurt her feelings, especially after she had gone to so much trouble.

"I love them," I told her, taking the bag. "These are great!"

"I used up all my allowance buying this stuff," she said proudly. "But I figured you needed it more than I did. After all, there's always plenty of cool music and cute guys right here in Sweet Valley. And if I need anything, I can always just beg Lila to buy it for me."

"Well, thanks, Jess. It was really sweet of you."

She beamed. "You're welcome." Suddenly she grabbed me in a big hug. "I'll miss you, Lizzie," she whispered in my ear.

I hugged her back hard, trying to keep my eyes from welling up. "I'll miss you too. A lot."

She pulled away after a few seconds, looking slightly embarrassed—she doesn't like mushy scenes much—and we headed back to Mom and Dad. After about a million more hugs and kisses and reminders, they noticed their time in the parking lot was running out. By then more people were showing up at the gate, including the adult chaperons from Rain Forest Friends who would be flying to Costa Rica with us. I told my family it was OK for them to head home, even though I could tell they didn't want to. (OK, except maybe for Jessica. She was yawning every two seconds and looking sleepy again.) So after another two million hugs and kisses—Steven even gave me a quick hug— they left.

I waved until I couldn't see them anymore. That was when I really felt like crying, but I reminded myself that I was about to set off on an adventure I would remember all my life and that I'd be helping a lot of people too. That cheered me up a little.

Then I saw the white plastic bag poking out of my carry-on. I really didn't want to bring along the stuff Jess had given me, but I didn't want to just throw it away either.

While I was trying to figure out what to do, a voice interrupted my thoughts.

"Hi! My name's Andy. Are you a Rain Forest Friend by any chance?"

I turned and saw a tall, skinny boy with glasses and reddish brown hair standing beside my chair. I smiled at him. "Hi, Andy. I'm Elizabeth. And yes, I'm part of the group."

"Me too." He sat down on the seat next to mine, dumping his duffel bag on the floor at his feet. He pushed his glasses farther up his nose. "I feel kind of dumb. I just spent ten minutes talking to a group of girls over by the soda machine before I realized they weren't part of our trip at all. They were just here on vacation from Canada." He shrugged and grinned sheepishly. "I went over and introduced myself, and I guess I was so excited, I just started talking. So I didn't figure out the truth until the girls started counting their change and talking about scraping together enough money to buy some magazines to read during the flight to Toronto."

"I think I saw those girls too." Then I smiled— Andy had just given me a great idea. If those Canadian girls wanted magazines, I knew where they could get some. . . .

"Hey, Andy," I said. "Would you do me a favor?"

"Sure," Andy replied. "Anything!"

"Can you keep an eye on my stuff for a minute? I—uh—need to go to the ladies' room."

"No problemo," he said, giving me a double-handed thumbs-up. "That's Spanish for 'no problem.' You can count on me, Elizabeth."

"Thanks." I took Jessica's gift and went back over to the spot behind the candy and soda machines. But the Canadian girls were nowhere in sight. For a second I just stood there, feeling disappointed.

*Maybe they went to the gift shop,* I thought. *Or maybe—*

I heard loud giggling coming from the ladies' room nearby.

*Aha!* I thought. *That must be them.* I was about to go into the ladies' room, but then I started to worry that they might think that a stranger giving them a gift in the bathroom was a little weird. So I leaned the bag against one of the candy machines, where the girls would be sure to see it as soon as they came out. Quickly I scribbled a note on the front of the bag: *To our Canadian visitors—have a great trip home!* Then I scooted back to my seat, grinning from ear to ear with the thought that I'd managed to do a good deed even before my trip got started.

When I got back to my seat, Andy was waiting for me. He smiled as I sat down. "Nobody came near your bags, Elizabeth," he said. "I watched them the whole time."

"Thanks, Andy." I smiled back. Andy was kind of goofy, but he seemed sweet. "So, how did you find out about this trip?"

Andy's face lit up. "Actually, it's a really interesting story. You see, my parents signed me up for an after-school Spanish class because I've always been really interested in foreign languages, and . . ."

I listened for a few minutes as Andy chattered on and on. But then suddenly I caught a flash of bright red out of the corner of my eye. I turned to see what it was.

It was a backpack, and it was being carried by a

boy who had just ambled into our section. He was about my age, kind of tall, with curly brown hair, hazel eyes, broad shoulders, and a sort of Jessica-like twinkle in his eye.

Even though I knew I was being rude to Andy (who luckily didn't seem to notice since he was caught up in a highly detailed description of his dog), I couldn't seem to stop looking at the new guy.

I'm not sure why. I mean, he was pretty cute. But I always thought that was one more thing that Jessica and I *don't* have in common—she gets totally distracted whenever she sees a guy who's even the slightest bit good-looking. I, on the other hand, happen to think there are lots of things that are more important than checking out guys, cute or not. In fact, just about the only guy I've ever thought was interesting in that more-than-a-friend way is Todd Wilkins. And lately I haven't even been thinking about him all that much, I guess because we've both been so busy—me with the end of the school year and then with planning this trip, and him with basketball and the swim team and other stuff.

But I definitely wasn't thinking about Todd Wilkins at that particular moment. Especially when the curly-haired guy dropped his red backpack on the first row of seats and glanced at one of the adult chaperons. "Yo," he called. "Is this where the Rain Forest amigos are hangin'?"

That got Andy's attention. He glanced over at the new guy. "He must be with us."

I nodded. I couldn't seem to tear my eyes away from the guy with the red backpack. I guess I must have been staring a little, because he noticed me. And then—he *smiled*. Needless to say, I was totally embarrassed. I couldn't believe he'd caught me gawking at him. I was about to turn away.

But then for some reason Jessica's voice popped into my head with one of her all-time favorite phrases: *"Go for it, Lizzie!"*

And suddenly I knew what she would do if she were in my place right now. If Jess had been staring at a cute guy and he'd caught her, she wouldn't just blush and turn away. No, she'd do something bold and daring, like wink at him or blow him a kiss. That made me wonder if maybe I hadn't been too shy around guys in the past. Maybe now that I was almost in eighth grade I needed to start being more daring, like Jessica. What harm could it do to try it out and see what happened?

All these thoughts raced through my head in about half a second. So the curly-haired guy was still smiling at me when I decided to follow my twin's advice and go for it. I'm not as bold as Jessica is, so I couldn't quite bring myself to wink or blow kisses. I decided to start simple: I smiled back.

*          *          *

I'm here! I'm really here!

I would have trouble believing it except that the sights and sounds and smells keep reminding me that it's true. We all felt it as soon as we got off the plane in San José, the capital of Costa Rica. It's always pretty warm in southern California, especially in the summer, so the hot, humid weather here wasn't too much of a shock. But just about everything else seems very different. Even the furniture in my hotel room looks exotic!

It's really beautiful here, even though we haven't left the city yet. Everything is green, flowers seem to be blooming absolutely everywhere, and I've already seen several kinds of birds and bugs I can't identify. Plus I spotted a cute little lizard on the wall of the airport as we were getting off the plane.

This has been one of the longest and most interesting days of my whole life. And it's only the first day of my trip!

One of the most interesting things about today was meeting J.P. That's his name—the curly-haired guy with the red backpack. After I smiled at him back at the airport, he came over to where Andy and I were sitting. "Hi there," he said. "Are you two Rain Forest Amigos too?"

Andy nodded and answered for both of us since

my throat had suddenly gone strangely dry. "My name's Andy, and this is Elizabeth."

"I'm J.P." He plopped down across the aisle from us, leaning back and spreading both arms out across the backs of the seats. "Nice to meet you."

"Where do you go to school?" Andy asked him.

"Greengrass Junior High," he replied. I had heard of the school—it's about fifteen miles from Sweet Valley. "I'll be in eighth grade next year," he added.

"Us too," Andy put in. "Right, Elizabeth?"

"Um, yeah," I said, glancing at J.P. out of the corner of my eye. For some reason I didn't want him to get the impression that Andy and I were—together. I mean, it was already obvious that J.P. was nothing like thoughtful, kind, serious Todd Wilkins. In other words, he wasn't what Jessica would have called my "type." He was more like Jessica's type—playful and fun loving. And cute, of course.

J.P. and Andy started chatting about how much fun this trip was going to be and stuff like that. I mostly just nodded and listened and let the two guys do the talking. I was feeling a little tongue-tied. Maybe I was just tired from getting up early.

Still, hadn't I just made a decision to try acting more like Jessica for a while? This was the perfect opportunity. Even if I had no real interest in J.P., that didn't mean I couldn't—well—*flirt* with him a little. It would be good practice.

As I was trying to remember some of the millions of flirtatious comments I'd heard Jessica make to guys in the past, we all heard a voice calling Andy's name. Andy turned and squinted across the seating area.

Suddenly his eyes lit up behind his glasses. "Hey," he said. "It's my friend Duane. I didn't know he was coming on this trip!" He gave J.P. and me a quick, apologetic smile. "We're in the science club together at school. I should go say hello."

I glanced across the room and saw a chubby boy wearing a *Star Trek* T-shirt waving eagerly in our direction.

"No problem," J.P. said.

Andy quickly gathered up his things, pausing just long enough to smile shyly at me. "Bye, Elizabeth," he said. "I hope I'll see you later." Without waiting for an answer, he rushed away toward his friend.

Then J.P. and I were alone. There was a moment of awkward silence while I desperately tried to come up with something witty and interesting to say. What on earth does Jessica find to talk to boys about anyway?

J.P. saved me. He started right in again where he'd left off, talking about the trip. I did my best to keep up. It went something like this—

J.P.: So what made you decide to join the Amigo crusade, Elizabeth?
*Me:* Uh, um, well, uh, it sounded like fun.

J.P.: Yeah, that's what I thought. I heard you can go
white-water rafting and surfing in Costa Rica
and all kinds of other cool stuff. Also, the
wildlife is supposed to be amazing. There are
136 types of snakes.
[OK, he didn't actually know the number—I
remembered it from my reading. Here's what
he really said:]

J.P.: I heard they have, like, about a million kinds of
snakes.

Me: Snakes are interesting. [Duh!]

J.P.: Uh, sure. So anyway, do you know anyone else
on the trip?

Me: No. Do you?

J.P.: Yeah, there are two or three other kids from
Greengrass here. [I think it was about this time
when he gave me this really amazing smile that
made him look cuter than ever.] But you're
probably way too cool for them, Elizabeth.

Me: [blushing like a lobster] Um, uh, uh . . .

Lucky for me, our boarding announcement
came right at that moment. J.P. and I pulled out our
boarding passes, and it turned out that we were in
different rows.

To tell the truth, I was kind of relieved. I wasn't
sure I was ready for a whole flight sitting next to
him and trying to make conversation. So far, my
experiment with acting more like Jessica wasn't
going too well. As I waited in line to board the

plane I suddenly thought of all sorts of clever, fascinating things I could have said to him.

But instead I'd just sat there like a dork and said almost nothing.

I tried not to think about that as I joined the line of students waiting to board.

I got on the plane and made my way down the narrow aisle. There were about twenty-five of us from the program on the plane, and we were all seated in the same section. I recognized the pretty dark-haired girl from the airport sitting by the window in my row. I sat down next to her and introduced myself.

"Hello," she said, looking me up and down as if she were trying to figure out whether I was worth talking to or not. "I'm Tanya. Where do you go to school?"

"Sweet Valley. I'm going into eighth grade." It felt kind of weird not to say "Sweet Valley Middle School," but she didn't seem to notice.

"I go to Greengrass Junior High. I'll be in eighth grade too."

"Greengrass? Really?" I said, thinking of J.P. "I heard that's a good school."

"One of the best in the state." She gave me a rather smug smile, then glanced down to check her seat belt. "It's not really bragging for me to say that, because I'm one of the people who helped make it so great."

"What do you mean?"

"I was the president of the seventh grade last year, so I got to help make a lot of the decisions that affected the whole school," she said. "I'll probably be president of the whole student council this year even though that office usually goes to a ninth-grader." She brushed a strand of dark hair off her cheek. "The principal already named me yearbook editor because I had the highest grades in the school last year."

I had to stop myself from rolling my eyes. For someone who didn't think she was bragging, Tanya sounded awfully conceited. Still, I couldn't totally blame her. It sounded like she had a lot to be conceited about.

I decided to change the subject. "What made you decide to come on this trip?" To be honest, I was pretty interested in hearing the answer. So far, Tanya didn't exactly seem like the sensitive, giving, do-gooder type.

"I won a state essay contest on Costa Rica," she said. "This trip was the grand prize. My parents don't have to pay a cent for it."

So that explained it.

"It's kind of silly, though," Tanya went on as the Fasten Seat Belts sign came on and the plane started to taxi toward the runway. "I mean, this trip would normally be a good learning experience for someone, but I already know just about everything there is to know about Costa Rica because of my research for the essay!" She shrugged and gave me that smug little smile again. "Still, I guess it will look good on my permanent record."

"Well, I'm sure that's true," I told her. "But I hadn't really thought about it that much. I was too excited about getting to help rebuild those flooded villages. Especially since the work I did with Houses for Humans was so fun and rewarding."

For the first time she looked slightly impressed. "You worked with Houses for Humans?"

I nodded. "I volunteered on a project with them last year."

"That's nice." Tanya settled back in her seat as the plane began to gather speed for takeoff. "I'm glad I'm not the only one with some building experience. I've worked on four Houses for Humans myself."

I felt my jaw drop. *Four* Houses for Humans? Was there anything Tanya hadn't accomplished? I couldn't help thinking that she should forget about eighth grade and just head straight for college right now. Or maybe the White House.

Still, even though I was impressed by the things Tanya had done, I didn't find myself liking her very much. In fact, the more I talked to her, the more I found myself getting annoyed with her. There was one thing she said that bugged me a lot. I guess I had mentioned something about the interesting plants and animals we were going to see in the rain forest.

"That should be interesting, of course," she said, even though she didn't sound like she really thought it was interesting at all. "But I'm not going to waste a lot of time looking for animals I can just go see in the zoo."

"But seeing them in the zoo isn't the same," I protested. "The exciting part will be finding them in their natural habitat. And spotting them will probably be a challenge, since I read that a lot of species are pretty shy, and others only come out at night, and—"

"Whatever." She rolled her eyes. "You can do all the animal spotting you want as long as you're not on my work team. Because I intend to make sure that I win the Outstanding Volunteer award when this trip is over, and that means my team is going to have to work hard."

"What award?" I asked.

"They present an award at the end of the trip," she explained. "To the person who did the most to help the project." She tossed her head so that her dark, thick hair bounced around her face. "But don't get your hopes up. I intend to win. If there's one thing I've learned, it's that being a winner is important. Very important. Even if *some* people don't seem to get that."

As she said that, she looked sort of ahead and across the aisle. I'm not positive, but it looked like she was staring right at J.P.!

It was weird. And there was more. A little while later I saw J.P. walk past on his way to the bathrooms at the back of the plane. On his way back he paused by my seat just long enough to smile at me. And I wouldn't swear to it, but I think he winked too! It was over so fast, I wasn't sure whether I had imagined the whole thing.

But that wasn't even the most interesting part. After he looked at me, he looked over at Tanya, who was taking a nap. His smile faded into a scowl, and he hurried back to his seat even though for a second I thought he was going to stop and talk to me.

I guess I shouldn't be surprised that they know each other. After all, they both go to Greengrass. But there seems to be something going on between them. Something even more mysterious than the puzzle in the mystery novel I read on the plane. What does it mean? I have no idea.

But I guess I have the next five weeks to find out.

# Two

◇

We were supposed to sleep in this morning to make up for our long, tiring day yesterday, but I was much too excited to sleep. I was wide awake by eight A.M. I couldn't wait to get started on our building—I almost wished we weren't stuck in the city for two more days of orientation and sightseeing, even though I was sure that would be interesting too.

I was tying my shoelaces when there was a knock on the door. I jumped up, a little startled.

"Who is it?" I called, glad that I had already gotten ten dressed and straightened my room. For a split second I was sure that it was J.P. at the door. I have no idea why. I hadn't seen much of J.P. since our talk at the airport—we had all been so exhausted after the long flight from the United States that most of us had headed straight for bed when we got here. I hadn't even thought about him very much. Still, his grinning face was the first thing that flashed into my mind right then.

It flashed out again quickly when I heard the response from the other side of the hotel door. "It's me, Elizabeth—Andy. Duane and I are heading down to breakfast. Do you want to sit with us?"

I sighed. "Sure, Andy," I called back, hurrying toward the door. "I'm ready."

Our program leaders, Marion and Robert, gave us a little "Rain Forest Friends" presentation at breakfast in the hotel dining room. They seem pretty cool. Marion is a graduate student; she's petite and pretty with auburn hair and a wide smile. Robert looks a few years older than Marion. He's one of the tallest and thinnest people I've ever met. His light brown hair sticks straight up in front, like Steven's sometimes does when he first wakes up. Somehow, though, I don't think Robert is the kind of person who cares much about how his hair looks (unlike Steven the Stud, ha-ha). He seems very nice but also very serious and thoughtful.

As we ate, the leaders stood and asked for our attention so they could tell us a little more about what we would be doing. Andy and Duane even stopped talking about the latest goings-on of the science club long enough to listen.

"Welcome, volunteers," Robert began. His voice was just as serious as the expression on his face. "You are about to embark on an adventure that will make a big difference in the lives of needy people."

"That's right," Marion went on. "Plus it will be a lot of fun if you approach it with the right attitude. I know you're all eager to help; otherwise you wouldn't have signed up for this trip. But it won't be all work and no play. You'll have plenty of opportunities to learn about Costa Rican culture and explore the rain forest you'll be working in. You'll probably see plants, birds, insects, and reptiles that you've never seen before, especially if you ask your host families for help in spotting them. By the way, Costa Ricans are known as *Ticos,* and I think you'll find the villagers you meet to be very friendly and helpful. All the host families you'll be staying with speak English, so you won't have any problems communicating with them or asking them for help. They can also translate between you and the other villagers."

Even though I was interested in what Marion was saying, I suddenly found my attention elsewhere. J.P. had just wandered into the room, yawning and scratching his head. He had obviously just rolled out of bed—his curls were wilder than ever

and there was a big pillow crease on his cheek—
but he still looked really cute.

Robert noticed him come in and frowned. But he
didn't say anything as J.P. scooted into the nearest
empty seat with a sheepish grin.

I frowned a little too. Everybody else had managed to get here on time. What was J.P.'s problem?
His lateness irritated me—maybe a little more than
it should have.

Besides, if J.P. had shown up on time, I could
have been sitting with *him* instead of Andy and
Duane.

Robert and Marion were still talking, and I
did my best to pay attention as they explained
that we would be divided into two construction
crews that would be working in two neighboring
villages. Actually, they're almost like two parts
of one big village since they're only about a
quarter of a mile apart, separated by a strip of
rain forest. So we'll all be able to visit each other
easily if our friends end up on the opposite
team.

Then they talked about the Outstanding
Volunteer award that Tanya had mentioned on
the plane. The plaque will be presented on the
last day of the trip to the student who has done
the most for the project. I had to admit that it
would be awfully cool to win an award like that.
It would make a nice souvenir, and every time I
looked at it, I would remember that I had done

something important with my summer vacation instead of just sitting around the pool.

As I was trying to figure out if the award would look better on my desk or hanging above my bed, I was distracted by a sudden motion near the door. I looked over and saw that it was J.P.— again. He had just loaded his spoon with pineapple chunks and was pretending he was going to shoot the boy across the table with it. Or maybe he really was planning to shoot it. I never found out because a sharp voice from the front of the room interrupted him.

"Young man," Robert snapped. "Are you paying attention?"

*Ha!* I thought. *Busted.*

J.P. dropped the spoon and sat up straight. "Uh, sorry about that," he said. "I was listening. Really. I'll test the airborne velocity of this pineapple— uh—later."

Robert glared at him for a second, giving J.P. the same look my father gives Steven when he's doing something really irritating. "I hope so," Robert said. "There won't be any time for goofing off on this trip. The villagers are counting on us to finish their new buildings before our five weeks are up. That's all the funding we have for this project. So if it doesn't get done now, it may not get done for a long time—especially since it's the rainy season and a lot of groups don't work now at all."

At last J.P. had the decency to look sheepish. "Sorry," he said.

Robert glared again and looked like he wanted to say something else, but Marion interrupted him. "Don't let Robert scare you too much," she said with a kind smile. "As I said before, there will be time for fun as well as work. But it *is* important to remember that our main goal is to complete our building projects before we leave. People are counting on us." She looked around at the whole group as she said it.

"And anyone who can't remember that," Robert added, "doesn't need to be here at all. I would hate to have to send any of you home." He looked as though he meant it too—the part about hating it as well as the part about sending us home. Robert was very serious, but I could tell he was a caring person. He glanced at J.P. once more before starting to describe the ecologically sound building materials we would be using.

I snuck a peek at J.P. too. He was sitting quietly, listening to Robert speak. I was glad that Robert had yelled at J.P. He deserved it. He had been goofing off and acting stupid when he should have been paying attention. But I couldn't help noticing one more time how cute he was, even with that pillow crease on his face.

I bit my lip and forced my gaze back to my breakfast, still confused. What did I think of J.P.? I didn't know. Even when I was annoyed with him, I couldn't help wanting to look at him and talk to him and get to know him better. Weird.

I snuck another look at J.P., who had loaded his spoon up with pineapple again. I rolled my eyes. Clearly Robert's little speech hadn't impressed him much. But I decided that Robert was right. The work was the reason we were all here. I didn't want to waste time on some guy who wasn't serious about the project and could only distract me. No matter how cute he was.

TUESDAY, 9:40 P.M.

I will never understand boys.

I know I already decided not to waste any more time thinking about J.P. But that's not so easy when he always seems to be popping up in front of me wherever I turn.

I hardly saw him yesterday. Instead I spent the day with the geek twins. Sorry, I know that isn't very nice. But Andy and Duane really are pretty nerdy. They're not just charter members of their school's science club. No, they're also really into the chess club and marching band and the Science Fiction Fan Society and the Young Bird-watchers' club too. Not that there's anything wrong with those things. But Andy and Duane sometimes seem to forget that not everybody is as fascinated with all that stuff as they are. Duane is much worse than Andy—actually,

Andy is really smart and has a good sense of humor. But when the two of them get together, *run for your life!*

So after breakfast this morning, when Marion told us to break into groups for a day of sightseeing, I was actually glad when Tanya grabbed my arm.

"You should be in our group, Elizabeth," she said. "You seem to be the only person I've met on this trip who knows anything at all about anything."

I shrugged, hiding a smile. I guessed some of the things I'd told her about myself on the plane must have sunk in after all. "OK," I said.

I smiled tentatively at the two girls standing behind Tanya. One of the girls smiled back. She was a little shorter than me, with hair almost the same shade of blond as mine, although hers was shorter and fluffier and kind of encircled her head like a halo. Her eyes were big and round and a really pure baby blue. Her face was kind of round too, and she had a button nose and a really big, open, friendly smile

"Hi," the blond girl said. "I'm Kate. This is Loren." She gestured at the third girl, who was very pale and thin. She didn't smile or nod or say "nice to meet you" or anything.

"Hi, I'm Elizabeth," I said, liking Kate immediately. I wondered how she had gotten roped into being in Tanya's group. "It's nice to meet you. Both of you," I added, glancing at Loren, who just shrugged.

Tanya tossed her head impatiently. "Come on, let's go," she commanded. "Marion is taking people to the museum, and I don't want to get lousy seats on the van."

I sighed. Spending the day with Queen Tanya wasn't looking like it would be any more fun than hanging out with the science nerds.

Still, I survived somehow. I even managed to have some fun, mostly thanks to Kate. She turned out to be just as friendly as she looked— and funny too. We spent half the day giggling over the way the guard at the museum kept saying *"pura vida, pura vida"* (which means "good" or something like that) every time we walked past him. Once we caught on, we started walking past his station every few minutes to see what he would do. He just kept saying *"pura vida, pura vida."* But I guess he realized we were joking around with him. Because when we were getting ready to leave the museum for good, he said, *"Hasta luego, mi hijitas. Pura vida!"* and winked at us.

Tanya wasn't the least bit amused by our little game with the guard. Jessica sometimes accuses me of being too serious, but I don't think Tanya has any sense of humor at all. And I have no idea what Loren thought about any of it. She didn't say more than three words the entire day.

After some more sightseeing we all headed back to the hotel dining room for dinner and some last minute instructions on life in the rain forest. The four of us found a table near the front of the room. Marion was sitting nearby, but Robert was nowhere in sight. Neither was J.P. Not that I cared.

Kate and I kept chatting as we ate, with Tanya throwing in a snotty comment once in a while. Loren just concentrated on her food. By now I knew that Kate went to the same school as J.P. and Tanya. I also knew that Kate had come on this trip mostly because she's crazy about animals and birds, and she's hoping to see lots of interesting species while she's here. But she's also looking forward to helping build homes for needy people. In fact, she's so serious about it that her big blue eyes fill up with tears every time she talks about it.

After we all had our food, Marion clapped for attention. She started off by explaining that tomorrow morning we would be taking a bus to a large town near our villages. Then she told us some of the things we would need to know to have a fun and safe time in the rain forest.

As she was describing several types of poisonous snakes we might encounter, J.P. came in—late again, I couldn't help noticing—with a group of three other boys. They were all laughing and talking loudly. It took them a second to realize that Marion was speaking. One by one the other three boys fell silent. But J.P. had his back to Marion, and I guess he was in the middle of telling a joke or something because he kept going.

". . . and so then the dog asked why they didn't make cowboy boots in his size. And . . ." J.P. looked confused as one of the boys gestured to him frantically. "And . . ." He looked around and spotted Marion frowning. "Oh." Suddenly J.P. realized that everyone in the room was staring at him. He grinned. "Ha-ha. Uh—oops."

Marion nodded sternly, although it looked to me as though she was struggling not to laugh. I rolled my eyes. J.P. was just lucky Robert wasn't around.

"Take your seats, boys," Marion said, and the four of them looked around for empty chairs. The other three boys found seats quickly, but J.P. was left standing.

I glanced at the empty seat between me and Loren, but I didn't say anything. *Let him find a seat at another table,* I told myself. *We don't need him throwing food at us.*

But Marion had just spotted the empty seat. "Here you go, J.P.," she called. "There's a free seat right there by Elizabeth Wakefield."

J.P. grinned. "Elizabeth Wakefield?" he exclaimed, loudly enough for the entire room to hear. "Great! I must be the luckiest boy in the whole wide world!" He clasped his hands to his chest and fluttered his eyelashes dramatically.

I blushed up to my scalp as Loren shot me a surprised glance and Kate giggled. Tanya was scowling. I didn't meet any of their eyes. I couldn't
believe J.P. had said that—what would everyone
think?

Most of the other kids were snickering as J.P.
loped across the room toward our table. He was
grinning broadly, as if he were very pleased with
himself. But he stopped short when he reached
the table and saw who else was there.

"Oh. Hi, Tanya," he said, his tone suddenly sub-
dued.

"Hello, J.P.," she replied icily. "It's nice to see
you've matured so much over the summer."

The sarcasm in her voice was so clear that no
one at the table could have missed it. But J.P. didn't
respond. Instead he sat down and turned to me
with a big smile. "So, Elizabeth," he said. "What
did you girls do today?"

I gulped. Having him sitting so close, looking so
cute, made me feel a bit light-headed. *You're not
Jessica*, I told myself firmly. *Get a grip!*

"Um, I think we'd better listen," I whispered,
gesturing to Marion, who had started speaking
again.

J.P. shrugged. "Whatever," he said. All of a
sudden he didn't seem very interested in talking
to me—not even to tease me or embarrass me.
He was too busy shooting dirty looks at Tanya,

who was pointedly ignoring him. Things stayed pretty much the same way until the meal ended, when J.P. slunk off with hardly a word to any of us.

It's like I said.

*I will never understand boys!*

# *Three*

We checked out of the hotel this morning and got ready to head out into the rain forest. The villages where we would be working were a pretty long way from the city, so we needed to get an early start. Marion and Robert explained that we would be staying overnight in San Sebastián, which is the largest town in that area, before heading on to our two villages, Valle Dulce and Gemelo, the next morning.

I was one of the first people on board the bus. I sat down near the front so I would have a good view out the windows. Tanya sort of smiled at me when she got on, and she took a step forward, obviously planning to sit with me. I guessed she'd gotten over that whole scene with J.P.—she'd seemed kind of angry about it all evening, even after J.P. left.

I smiled back weakly, feeling trapped. I had been hoping to sit with Kate, but I didn't want to make Tanya mad. I began preparing myself for a long, dull ride spent listening to her talk about herself.

"Heads up!" someone shouted.

It was J.P. He hopped up the bus steps and pushed past Tanya. Actually, he hardly touched her at all as he went by, although by the way she jumped back, you would have thought he'd poked her with a red-hot branding iron or something.

"Hi, Elizabeth," he said, stopping by my seat. He gave me a huge grin and made a sort of little half bow. "Is this seat taken?"

"Um, no," I said, feeling flattered and kind of bashful at the same time in spite of myself. "I guess not. Go ahead."

He sat down, and then he turned and sort of smirked at Tanya. She just stalked past and sat down a few seats behind us.

That made me feel kind of weird. I don't like making enemies, especially with someone I might have to work with for the next five weeks. And whatever was going on between J.P. and Tanya, I didn't want to end up in the middle of it.

But I also felt strange because I still didn't know quite what to think about J.P. I kept flip-flopping back and forth in my mind. One second I was determined to avoid him since he was so distracting and goofy. The next I would find myself thinking that I should get to know him better. I was realizing that there was something really cool about J.P., and I'm not just talking about how cute he was. It was something about his personality—the way he wasn't afraid to say and do whatever he wanted. Maybe some of the stuff he did annoyed me—like being late. But I could imagine what Jessica would say about that if she were here: *Give him a break, Lizzie. He's just having fun!*

Maybe that was true. After all, even if we were here to work, we were also here to have fun. J.P. really knew how to do that. Did I? Or was I more like Tanya, who was so busy worrying about her junior-high transcript and being mature that she forgot to enjoy herself?

Next to me J.P. was craning his neck around, looking behind us. "No offense, Elizabeth," he said. "But this is a really lame seat. Come on, let's move to the back."

I hesitated. Like I said, I had chosen that seat so I would have a good view. We wouldn't be able to see out nearly as well from the back, and besides, I had read that a lot of the roads in Costa Rica aren't even paved, so I was afraid it would be really bumpy back there.

I opened my mouth to explain all of that to J.P. But he was already halfway down the aisle. "Wait!" I called.

He turned around for a second. "Come on!" he called to me. "Backseat is where it's at!"

For a second I almost stayed where I was. Kate would be here soon; she could sit with me. Who needed J.P.? But I felt my legs moving on their own, standing up and stepping out of the seat. *I just don't want to be rude*, I thought. I scooted out of the seat and hurried down the aisle, trying not to notice the dirty look that Tanya flashed me as I walked past her seat. When I reached the back, J.P. hopped up and offered me the window seat, which I gladly accepted.

Then we got started. I was a little nervous about finding things to say to J.P., but as it turned out, I didn't have to worry. He kept me laughing with all sorts of jokes and stories. I actually found myself having fun listening to him. True, he was kind of silly and loud. But he was smart too. And he seemed to be pretty nice—like none of his goofing around was really meant to be mean.

Still, my opinion of him kept doing that flip-flopping thing.

He told me about an art project he'd done last year. *He's artistic!* I thought.

Then he started describing some of the practical jokes he'd played on his older sisters. *What a jerk*, I thought.

He asked me a lot of questions about my work for the school newspaper and acted really interested in what I told him. *Hmmm. Maybe he's OK.*

Then I told him about Jessica, and after he found out I was a twin, he decided to start calling me Bob, as in Bobbsey twin. *Aargh!* I thought.

Flip. Flop. I just couldn't make up my mind one way or the other.

Between laughing at J.P.'s silly stories, getting annoyed at his immature comments, and watching the interesting scenery, the first hour or two of our bus trip flew by. But after a while I noticed that the ride was getting bumpier and the road was getting narrower as we made our way through some mountains. We came to an area that went up and down steeply every few minutes and around a lot of hairpin turns, and I found myself getting kind of nervous, especially since the bus driver didn't slow down much for most of the turns. In fact—and I might have been wrong about this—he seemed to be *speeding up* for the turns.

I said something about it to J.P. He didn't seem scared at all, though.

"Don't worry," he said, making his voice as deep as he could and flexing the muscles in one arm. "I'm a manly man, and I won't let anything bad happen to a pretty lady like you."

I rolled my eyes. I wasn't exactly counting on J.P. to come to my rescue if the bus crashed. But then I realized belatedly that he had called me pretty. I started blushing madly. I didn't want him to see, so I turned my face toward the window.

That was when I saw it. We were careening straight toward a steep drop-off, going way too fast to stop!

My heart froze. I was too scared to scream. Instead I dug my fingernails into the back of the seat in front of me and sort of whimpered. This was it. We were all going to end up horribly mangled in some Costa Rican hospital! I tried to squeeze my eyes closed, but they were glued to the cliff we were about to go over.

Meanwhile J.P. noticed my look of terror and leaned over to see what I had seen. But when he saw the drop-off, he just grinned and shouted "Yee-ha!" at the top of his lungs. He grabbed me, wrapped both arms around me, and squeezed. "I'm protecting you!" he yelled right in my left ear.

For a second I thought he was crazy. Then, as the driver spun the steering wheel and I realized it was just another hairpin curve, I started to feel embarrassed for panicking like that. Then I forgot all about that feeling when I remembered J.P.'s arms were still around me. That made me feel flustered, and confused, and . . . well, I wasn't sure what else.

He loosened his grip a little so he could pull back and look at me.

"This is great, isn't it, Bob?" he said. "Sort of like a ride at Disneyland."

I frowned and opened my mouth to disagree. I had really been scared, and I didn't think it was fun at all. Then the bus swooped around another curve, throwing me toward J.P. His arms tightened again, and he laughed.

I did too. I couldn't help it—his laugh was catching.

*Go for it, Lizzie!* Jessica's words floated through my mind again. I didn't have to think too hard to figure out what she would do if she were me.

Suddenly I found myself thinking that maybe being scared had its advantages. Maybe J.P. was a goofball, but he was really cute—and his arms *were* awfully strong. . . . "Oh, no!" I cried, glancing out the window. "Here comes a sharp one!"

It was stupid, I know. Those roads probably were really dangerous. But I truly had forgotten that for a minute. Suddenly I felt as though I'd gotten a little bit of insight into why Jessica and her friends do all the harebrained things they do.

I guess that sometimes it's easy to get caught up in the moment.

*THURSDAY, 11:15 P.M.*

So much happened today, Diary! I'll write about everything in a second, but first I have to get one thing off my chest:

*Tanya is a total jerk!*

I feel much better now. OK, so let me start from the beginning.

We got to San Sebastián right on schedule. It was a colorful, bustling town, much smaller than the city, but still full of interesting people and things to see. We had just enough time to eat dinner and take a look around before collapsing in exhaustion.

I woke up early again this morning. But when I looked at the second bed in the room, I noticed that Loren was already up and gone. I wasn't sorry about that. I'd been disappointed when Marion had assigned us a room together. And Loren had hardly said two words to me as we were getting ready for bed. Still, I knew it could have been worse. I could have been stuck with Tanya. I'd much rather room with someone who doesn't talk at all than someone who only talks about herself.

I was pulling on my shorts when the door to the room flew open. I glanced up, expecting it to be Loren.

"Oops!" Kate cried, blushing. She quickly closed the door again. "Sorry, I guess I forgot to knock! I was too excited," she said from the hall.

I hurriedly fastened my shorts and called out, "That's OK, come on in!" I smiled as she opened the door again. *At last, someone to talk to who might actually talk back,* I thought wryly. "I'm almost ready. What's up?"

"Good news." Kate perched on the edge of Loren's bed while she waited for me to tie my shoelaces. "Marion and Robert just posted our assignments in the lobby, and you and I are in the same village—Valle Dulce. Not only that, we'll both be staying with the same host family, the Herreras!"

"That's great!" I exclaimed. "Do you know who else is in our village? What about Loren and Tanya?"

Kate wrinkled her nose. "Loren's with us. But Tanya got the other village, thank goodness." She giggled. "Sorry, that's kind of mean."

"It's OK," I said quickly as I finished tying my shoes and stood up. "I understand, believe me." I was relieved that Tanya and I were in different villages. Maybe now I wouldn't have to hear any more about her perfect grades and prize-winning essays.

I couldn't help wondering which village J.P. was in. But I didn't want to ask Kate and let her know that I cared. Not that I did—not much anyway. I was just curious. "Why don't we head down to breakfast?" I suggested. "Maybe on the way we can stop by the lobby so I can check out the good news for myself." *And see exactly who else is on the list for Valle Dulce,* I added silently.

Kate nodded agreeably. "Let's go!"

When we reached the lobby, there was a small group of kids clustered in front of the list. I stood on tiptoe, trying to see past the girl in front of me. I scanned the names on the Valle Dulce side quickly, taking note of mine and Kate's. A little farther down I spotted another familiar name, and my heart soared.

"Yo, Bob," a voice called behind me at that moment. It was J.P. "Which village did you get?"

"Valle Dulce," I said. "And stop calling me Bob." I turned to face him and saw that Andy and Duane were standing with him.

J.P. grinned. "Me too! Andy and I are bunking together. Right, dude?" He punched Andy lightly on the arm.

Andy nodded, but he looked kind of sad. Duane looked even sadder, and I guessed that meant he was in the other village—Tanya's village. *Poor guy,* I thought.

I glanced back at J.P. He was bouncing up and down on the balls of his feet. "This is it," he crowed. "We're almost there. Time to get down to business."

I gulped, realizing that he was exactly right, although maybe not in the way he meant. Here I was, all aflutter because I was on the same team with a cute guy—a cute guy who insisted on calling me *Bob,* no less. But was that really what I ought to be feeling? Shouldn't I be more concerned with being on a team where all the members were serious and dedicated to our project? We had a real job to do, and nothing should stand in the way of that. Maybe I would have been better off if J.P. had ended up with Tanya. Welcome to my flip-flop world.

Kate, for one, didn't seem to share my concerns. "This is going to be so much fun!" she cried, clapping.

J.P. grinned at her. "You said it," he declared. "And I'm ready for it. Fun's my middle name!"

Just then Marion strode into the lobby. "I'm glad to see you found our list," she said. "But you'd better go grab some breakfast—the bus will be here to pick you up in half an hour. We'll stop at Valle Dulce first, then continue on to Gemelo. Got it? Good. Then let's eat. You'll need to keep up your strength for all that building!" She grinned at us, then led the way into the dining room.

Half an hour later we were in line, waiting to board the bus. I was standing between Kate and Andy, and J.P. and Duane were in front of us. Loren and Tanya were standing with a couple of other girls nearby. Marion and Robert were outside the bus door, checking off our names on a clipboard.

"Here we are, Cap'n," J.P. announced as we passed the adults. "Right on time."

"That's kind of a miracle, actually," Marion said with a chuckle, glancing at her watch. "Things in

Costa Rica hardly ever run on schedule."

"I guess that's why *you* like it here so much, J.P.," I joked. "After all, you're always late."

The others laughed, but J.P. turned and cocked one eyebrow at me quizzically. "Oh, really?" he said with a slight smirk. "I didn't realize you were paying such close attention to my schedule, Bob."

I blushed, wanting to sink into the ground. I should have known better than to try to tease J.P. He always had a perfect comeback.

I smiled weakly and moved forward to climb onto the bus. I sat down next to Kate, and J.P. slid into the seat behind us.

"Hey, Bob," he said, speaking more quietly than usual. "I was just kidding back there. I hope I didn't embarrass you or anything."

I shrugged quickly. The last thing I wanted was for him to think I was some kind of hypersensitive jerk. "No big deal," I said. "Hey, J.P., did you know that Kate is a really great horseback rider?"

After that the half-hour ride to Valle Dulce passed quickly. Kate and I watched the fascinating Costa Rican scenery slide past the bus windows. J.P. sat behind us, cracking jokes the whole time. Andy and Duane were across the aisle, still trying to come to terms with the fact that they weren't going to get to spend the entire trip together. I think they were trying to cram a whole five weeks' worth of *Star Trek* discussions into that half-hour ride. Meanwhile Tanya and Loren were sitting a couple of seats ahead. Every time there was a burst of laughter from our group, Tanya shot us a dirty look over her shoulder.

When our bus pulled up in front of Valle Dulce's town hall, it seemed as though the entire population of the village was there, waiting to greet us.

"Those of you continuing on to Gemelo, feel free to get off and look around, stretch your legs," Robert called as the driver pulled over. "It will take us a while to get all the luggage sorted out anyway."

The Herreras were the first ones to rush forward to greet us as we climbed off the bus. Robert pointed to Kate and me, and before I knew it, we were totally mobbed. At first I wasn't even sure how many of them there were because they talked so quickly and jumped around so much. But I soon figured out that there were six people in the family, two parents and four kids. (There's also a grandmother who lives with them, but I didn't meet her until later, when I got to their house.) Veronica and Jorge are the oldest Herrera kids— they're around my age. Eugenia is six and Ricardo is four, and they're both adorable, with big brown eyes and dark hair.

Mr. and Mrs. Herrera (actually, I guess that should be Señor and Señora Herrera) smiled at

us, then stepped away to talk to Marion and
Robert. Meanwhile Veronica was grinning at us,
looking excited.

"Awesome to meet you, Elizabeth and Kate,"
she said. "We are going to have a majorly cool
time in Costa Rica. You will like our house too—
my parents are kind of clueless, but they are not
bad for old fogies. Anyway, I am totally psyched
that you have come here to rebuild our community center; I loved watching American TV,
movies, and music videos there. It even had a
VCR—I was so very bummed when it got destroyed by the floods."

Veronica talked really fast, and for a while I
thought we weren't going to be able to get a word
in edgewise, but she finally had to pause to take a
breath. I opened my mouth to say something
about how happy I was to be there. I was also
going to compliment her on how well she spoke
English—she hardly had an accent at all. And no
wonder—from all the American slang she'd
packed into a few sentences, I guessed she had
watched a *lot* of American TV! I thought it was
cute how she had picked up all those words and
expressions.

But before I could say a word, Tanya spoke up.
She had gotten off the bus and was standing
nearby, listening to the whole thing.

"Give me a break," she said scornfully, looking
down her nose at Veronica. "We're here to rebuild

your village, not to talk about American TV. And we definitely don't need to practice our *awesome* American slang from the 1980s."

Veronica looked mortified, and I was *furious!* What was Tanya's problem? Veronica was being nice and friendly, and Tanya had just made her feel like a total idiot.

J.P. was listening too, and I guess he was thinking the same thing I was because he jumped right in.

"Yo, Veronica, your English is awesome," he said, totally ignoring Tanya. "Where did you learn to speak it so well?"

I struggled to suppress a laugh. Awesome? Since when did J.P. use a word like that? Ever since Tanya had used it to make Veronica feel stupid, I guessed. J.P. is so cool sometimes—of course he would find a way to use Tanya's rude comments against her.

Veronica gave him a shy and kind of grateful look. "I have learned some in school. But mostly I learn by watching TV and movies at the community center. I mean, I used to before the flood."

"Well, you must be *majorly* brainy to pick it up that way," J.P. said sincerely. "When it comes to Spanish, I'm totally clueless. I can't even count to ten—no matter how many times I watched them do it on *Sesame Street* when I was a kid! How does it go—*uno, dos,* trees, quarter, sink. . . ."

Veronica giggled. "I have often seen *Sesame*

*Street* at the community center," she said. "My little sister and brother love Elmo, but personally, I think Cookie Monster is awesome. He is my favorite character."

"Mine too," I said. "Cookie is *totally* awesome." I smiled at J.P. Hey, I know just as much slang as anybody.

Tanya may be a jerk, but she's no fool. She caught on pretty quick. She shook her head and muttered something under her breath about how immature we all were. Then she stomped away and climbed back on the bus.

I didn't shed a single tear when she left.

After the bus headed off toward Gemelo, the Herreras took Kate and me to their house for lunch, which was great—and very filling! It turns out that in Costa Rica, lunch is the most important meal of the day. We had all kinds of typical Tico dishes, including *chorreados*, which are sort of like corn cakes, *arroz con pollo*, which is a chicken dish, and lots of other things.

Delicious!

After we finished eating, Veronica and Jorge pointed the way toward the construction site. Marion had asked the whole group to meet there for one last set of instructions and information. Meanwhile Robert would be talking to Tanya and Duane and the others over at the other village.

About half the others were already there when Kate and I arrived. There were about a dozen kids in our group, including Kate, me, J.P., Andy, and Loren. The two boys weren't there yet, but I spotted Loren sitting in the front row next to a girl named Tiffany. "This is so exciting," Kate whispered, her eyes sparkling as we sat down on the ground behind a couple of guys named Ricky and Will.

I nodded and started to answer. But at that moment Andy plopped down right next to me. "Hi, Elizabeth," he said. "Hi, Kate."

Before we could answer, another voice broke in. "Yo, Bob!" J.P. exclaimed breathlessly, hurrying over and taking a seat behind me. "Here I am—on time for once. Right?"

I rolled my eyes. "Right. And don't call me Bob."

J.P. just grinned and then said hi to Kate.

"That was really nice, J.P.," Kate told him sincerely. "What you did back there for Veronica, I mean."

J.P. waved his hand. "No big deal," he said. "Tanya's evil. I didn't want her to ruin things."

Andy turned to me and said quietly, "I'm glad we're on the same team, Elizabeth. I'm looking forward to working with you."

"Thanks, Andy. I'm looking forward to it too." His steady gaze was making me a little uncomfortable. Why was he looking at me like that? And did he have to sit so close—practically in my lap? Didn't he know he was being kind of rude? Either he had no social skills whatsoever, or—suddenly a terrible thought occurred to me. *Uh-oh,* I thought. *Does Andy have a—a* crush *on me?*

I didn't have much time to think about it since Marion had just arrived and called for our attention. I sighed and settled back to listen. I could worry about this latest case of weird boy behavior later.

Marion told us that we would be rebuilding the community center that was destroyed in the floods. She wanted us to elect a leader to act as our foreman and oversee the construction (the kids in the other village will be doing the same thing) since she and Robert won't be staying in the villages with us all the time. We'll be under the supervision of our host families and a local builder who will stop by occasionally to help us.

The first thought that popped into my mind was that J.P. would make a fantastic foreman. I mean, he has a way of making everything—even riding over dangerous roads in a creaky old bus—seem like tons of fun. Plus he's obviously smart and talented. And if he had such an important job to do, maybe he would even calm down a little and stop goofing around so much. Perfect.

I guess Kate must have thought so too because as soon as Marion asked for nominations, she stuck up her hand and suggested J.P.

I looked over at him, expecting him to be psyched, but he was frowning.

"Sorry," he said, sitting up straight. "The whole leader thing isn't really my scene."

"But J.P.!" Kate's big blue eyes were wider than ever. I could tell she was as surprised at his reaction as I was. "You're perfect for the job. You did that scale model city in art class last year." She turned to look at the rest of us. "It won first prize in our school's fine arts fair."

"Sorry," J.P. said again. "I'm just not into being the boss." He shrugged. "Besides, an art project is one thing. A real building is another. I don't have that kind of experience."

Marion was nodding. "All right," she said. "We're not going to draft you for the job if you don't want it. And actually, your comments gave me a good idea about who might make an appropriate foreman." She turned and smiled straight at me. "I understand from her application that Elizabeth Wakefield has done some work with Houses for Humans. Is that right, Elizabeth?"

"Yes," I replied. I was about to go into more detail about the project I worked on (mostly to explain that I had just done whatever the foreman told me to do, since Marion kind of made it sound like I practically built the whole house myself), but Marion wasn't finished.

"In addition to her hands-on construction experience, Elizabeth appears to be a natural-born leader. She gets straight A's in school, she was editor of her sixth grade paper, she . . ."

Marion went on listing my achievements. But I wasn't listening too closely because by now I realized that Marion wanted *me* to be the foreman. And I wasn't sure how I felt about that.

I like being in charge—sometimes. But I'm not like Jessica, who always wants to be the center of attention. When I pictured myself building homes in Costa Rica, I had imagined working as part of a team, side by side with the other kids. Not bossing them around and being responsible for the whole project. It was sort of scary to think about having a whole village counting on me to build them a new community center. Granted, it was just a one-room structure, but it was still a real building.

But I didn't know how to say that without sounding like a big baby. And somehow I didn't think copying J.P.'s little speech was going to work for me—especially not after all the things Marion had just said about me. I smiled weakly.

"Um, OK," I said. "If you really think I can do it. And if nobody else wants the job."

"You'll do great," Marion assured me. She dug in the pocket of her khaki shorts and brought out a key. "This is the key to the office shack. It's right over there." She pointed to a shed on the other side of the clearing, then turned back to address the group. "The rest of you are dismissed. Enjoy your first evening in Valle Dulce, but try not to have *too* much fun." She grinned. "You've got to be up bright and early tomorrow to get down to work."

The other kids scattered as Marion brought me the key to the shed. She said it was where I would find the tools, materials, instruction manuals, and all the other stuff I'd need for *my* community center building.

Yikes! What had I gotten myself into? It was just lucky I had all those helpful hints from the Coco's Construction Concepts Web page. And I reassured myself with the thought that Robert and Marion would be dropping by, not to mention the local builder.

As Marion hurried off I turned the key in the lock and stepped into the office shack. I looked around. There was a desk in one corner with a little battery-operated fan, a lamp, some pens and papers and stuff, and even a portable CD boom box. Nearby was a wall rack containing a bunch of tools, and half of the shack was filled with large piles of lumber, scraps of metal, old tires, and other junk.

I locked up again and wandered back toward the Herreras' house. I figured I should offer to help prepare dinner and see if I could be useful in any other ways. It seemed the least I could do since the family was letting me live in their home for more than a month.

On my way down the little path leading through the strip of forest between the site and the main part of the village, I ran into J.P. He grinned at me, and before I knew it, I was in the middle of another weird boy conversation that made me question my whole opinion of him once again. It went something like this:

J.P.: Hey, Bob. How's it going?
*Me:* Don't call me Bob.
J.P.: [with a goofy grin] Sorry. I guess I'd better start calling you Foreman Bob now, huh? So where are you off to, Foreman Bob?
*Me:* I was just going back to the Herreras' to see if I can help with dinner.
J.P.: Cool! Maybe you can get extra credit with your home ec teacher for it.
*Me:* You're so funny.
J.P.: Hey, are you sure you should be talking to me, Foreman Bob? I mean, I'm just a regular guy, not a superachiever like you.
*Me:* What?
J.P.: Maybe you should talk to Andy instead. You guys can discuss the latest world chess championships.

I was starting to get really annoyed by that point. Maybe he was just kidding around as usual, but it didn't seem that funny this time. He was acting as if he thought I considered myself better than him, kind of like Tanya. I guess it was because of all that stuff Marion had said about me.

But if J.P. was waiting around for me to apologize for being a good student, he had a long wait ahead of him. I happen to like learning. Besides, being smart doesn't mean you can't have a sense of humor or that you don't know how to have fun. It doesn't mean I'm anything like Tanya. I'm starting to think I was right when I decided to stay away from him. In fact, I'm not going to write about him or even think about him anymore.

I know, I'm flip-flopping again.

But I mean it this time. I'm going to start right now. After all, there are lots of better things to think about. Like the local wildlife, for instance. Kate's already spotted about twenty kinds of birds and ten kinds of reptiles. She even caught a glimpse of something she thought was a coati, which is sort of like the Costa Rican version of a raccoon.

Sometimes it's hard to believe that I'm really in Costa Rica, but every time I look around, the interesting new sights convince me. I wish I had a tape recorder to catch the sounds that start to come out of the rain forest when the sun goes down. It's as if there are a million kinds of bugs, frogs, and who knows what else (monkeys? I heard there are some here, though I haven't seen any yet) all joining in a big chorus, chirping and croaking and screeching away. Over dinner tonight Mrs. Herrera said the sound gets almost deafening sometimes, but they're all so used to it, they hardly notice.

*    *    *

Despite my vow to forget about J.P., I woke up this morning thinking about him. I just couldn't get that conversation—if you could call it a conversation—out of my mind. It really bugged me that J.P. seemed to be judging me, even in a joking way, because of what Marion had said.

Kate and I got dressed in the spare bedroom in the Herreras' house, which is where we're staying while we're here. It's a small room, not much bigger than the bathroom Jess and I share at home. But it's cozy and welcoming, thanks to the colorful curtains and bedspreads, several carved wooden knickknacks, an embroidered wall hanging of a rain forest scene, and other homey touches.

Kate yawned and glanced at her watch as she reached for her shoes. "It's almost time for breakfast at the construction site. Are you psyched for our first day?" she asked cheerfully.

I sighed. "Well, the breakfast part doesn't sound too bad," I muttered. I wasn't looking forward to seeing J.P.—or starting my job as foreman, thanks to his teasing.

Kate's big blue eyes clouded over with concern. "What do you mean, Elizabeth?"

"I don't know." I finished buckling the belt on my shorts. "I think I would be more excited if someone else was foreman and I was just a worker like everyone else."

Kate gazed at me. "You mean you don't want to be foreman?"

"It's not that," I told her. Then I remembered that she goes to the same school as J.P. and Tanya. "How well do you know J.P.?" I asked.

She shrugged and sat down on the edge of her bed. "Not that well," she said. "We go to the same school, but we hardly have any classes together. He's in all the advanced classes because he's supposed to be some kind of genius."

"Really?" That didn't make much sense to me. If J.P. was so smart in school, why had he been so down on my grades and everything?

Kate nodded. "That's what they say. I guess that's why they keep him in those classes even though he's practically flunking out of most of them." She shrugged again. "If you ask me, he's kind of a slacker. Or maybe I should say partyer. He loves to have fun, and he hates to be serious or work at anything he doesn't think is interesting. And he doesn't think much about school is interesting except maybe art class. He's really good at that."

"Oh." Now it all made much more sense. And suddenly I had another thought. "Is that why Tanya doesn't seem to like him? Because he goofs off too much?"

Kate giggled. "Not exactly. She and J.P. used to be a couple. They went out through half of seventh grade. But they broke up at the end of the year."

"Oh." That explained a lot. A *lot*. Although I had a hard time picturing how a mismatched pair like J.P. and Tanya could get together in the first place.

The Herrera kids were still sleeping when we left our room, and Mr. and Mrs. Herrera were getting ready to leave for San Sebastián, where they both have office jobs. Kate and I said good-bye to them and headed over to the construction site, where Marion had laid out a picnic for us. She told us that most of the food had been prepared for us by the villagers. I could believe it. It was all just as delicious as yesterday's lunch had been. My favorite dish was made with rice and beans and called *gallo pinto*, which Marion explained was the Tico national breakfast.

Robert came by in a four-wheel-drive vehicle to pick up Marion at around nine o'clock. Before they left, they called us all into the clearing in front of the construction site for a few last-minute announcements. They said they'll be stopping by our two villages (oh, and by the way—Robert happened to mention that Tanya was elected team leader at her village. Big fat hairy surprise!) as often as they can to see how we're doing.

It turns out there are at least half a dozen groups of kids working in different parts of this area, not just our two. Marion and Robert have to help them all. That's why they're not staying full-time in Valle Dulce or Gemelo. They'll be in San Sebastián and on the road for most of the next five weeks.

Anyway, they told us the main shipment of construction materials for the buildings is on the way. It was supposed to arrive before we did, but I guess it's hard to keep roads clear in the rain forest, and the truck was delayed. Since the trucking company is donating their services, they aren't exactly sure when they can get the stuff here now. It could be tomorrow, it could be next week.

Robert said it shouldn't affect us much. We'll need to spend the first couple of days preparing the ground and building the foundation, and after that we have enough wood stacked behind the office shack to get most of the framing done. The local builder would come help us when the materials arrived. Until then, I was in control.

Before they left, the adults also mentioned something interesting about Tanya's village, Gemelo. A lot more homes there were affected by the floods than here, so the Rain Forest Friends didn't want to ask the villagers to put up the teen workers in their houses. Instead they set up a bunch of tents for them to sleep in. It sounds like the tents are pretty snazzy—each person gets his or her own private one, they have canvas floors and screened zip-up windows to keep the mosquitoes and other bugs out, stuff like that—but the point is, they're still tents. So I guess those of us in Valle Dulce really lucked out!

The rest of the day went well. I was nervous about getting started, but the rest of the crew was a lot of help. A boy named Ty had helped his father with the foundation of their new garage. A girl named Sumi had some good ideas about organizing the materials. And Andy was great at translating the directions that are in Spanish.

Otherwise not much happened. The good news was that J.P. stopped calling me Bob. The bad news was that he called me Madame Foreman all day instead, and at lunch he kept offering to pour me more juice and serve me more food in this ridiculous French waiter voice. He even offered to chew my food for me, which cracked up everyone except me (and Loren, who smiles about as often as she talks). Ugh! I really don't know what I should do about him. I wish Jessica were here to help me come up with a plan.

# *Four*

◇

Boy, Diary—has this been a long, confusing, exciting, weird, interesting, and sometimes even fun day!

Our second day of work went pretty well. I managed to ignore most of J.P.'s teasing and goofing around, and the rest of the team worked really hard. We got a ton of work done on the foundation, and I was sure we'd be ready to start framing soon. By the time Kate and I headed back to the Herreras' for dinner, we were dirty, hot, hungry, and exhausted.

We gobbled down the food Mrs. Herrera had prepared for us, then headed off to shower and change clothes. Veronica and Jorge had promised to show us around the rain forest when we were ready.

When I got back to the kitchen, I was surprised to find a small crowd gathered there. Mr. and Mrs. Herrera were bustling around near the stove. Sitting at the big wooden table where we'd eaten dinner were Veronica, Jorge, their grandmother, and a clean-scrubbed Kate. But they weren't the only ones. J.P. and Andy were there too, along with the Costa Rican family they were staying with.

"Oh," I said when I came in. "Hi, everyone."

As soon as she saw me, Veronica jumped up.

"Cool!" she cried. "Here is Elizabeth. Kate and the guys and I were just about to come search for you. These dudes are dying to check out the forest." She waved a hand in the direction of J.P. and Andy. "So they're coming with us, okeydokey?"

I hesitated. I had been looking forward to exploring the rain forest with Kate and the Herrera kids. But it didn't sound quite as appealing when I knew I'd have to put up with J.P.'s jokes and Andy's lovesick stares. "Maybe we should do it tomorrow," I suggested. "Kate and I should probably stick around and help clean up from dinner."

Jorge, Veronica's brother, rolled his eyes. "Not necessary, Elizabeth," he said. He has a stronger Spanish accent than his sister, but his English is really good too. "It is finished already."

Mrs. Herrera turned away from the sink, where she was filling a teakettle with water while her husband set some pastry-type things on a platter nearby. "Don't worry, Elizabeth," she said. "Go along and have fun."

"But—," I started to protest.

J.P. interrupted. "Hey, maybe dragging Bo—uh, I mean Elizabeth out to the rain forest isn't such a good idea. I mean, there are lots of bugs and things out there." He grinned at me. "Snakes too. A lot of girls are scared of that stuff."

I scowled at him. Bugs aren't my favorite thing in the world, but they don't bother me the way they do some people—like Jessica's friend Ellen Riteman, for instance. Ellen is so scared of spiders that if she sees one, even a teeny-tiny one twenty feet away, she screams at the top of her lungs and jumps up on the nearest piece of furniture as fast as she can. I know because once she tried to get away from a daddy longlegs by jumping onto the picnic table behind our house, but then she saw that there were *two* daddy longlegs on the table right next to her! She jumped off so fast that she ended up spraining her ankle.

I'm not like that. Bugs don't bother me. And I'm certainly not afraid of snakes unless they're poisonous. I was actually looking forward to seeing some of the interesting varieties I'd read about.

Somehow, though, I didn't think J.P. would be impressed if I put it that way. So I just said, "I'm not afraid of a few bugs and snakes. Are you?"

"No way." He threw me a challenging look. "But I don't think I believe you. If you're not afraid, then prove it. Come to the rain forest with us right now."

"I don't have to prove anything." I was starting to feel really annoyed at his attitude. I turned to Mrs. Herrera again. "Are you sure I can't help with anything?" I offered. "I can finish making tea or coffee if you like, so you can sit down and relax."

"Me too," Andy spoke up earnestly. "I don't mind staying here with Elizabeth and helping out." I rolled my eyes. I guess it was sweet of him to offer, but I wasn't really looking for an excuse to spend quality time with Andy.

Mrs. Herrera just laughed and patted me on the shoulder. "I told you, *macha*, everything is under control here. Run along with the others and have some fun. You too, Andy." (By the way, I asked Veronica later about what her mother had called me. Veronica explained that Ticos love to give people nicknames, especially descriptive ones. Mrs. Herrera had called me *macha*, which means "blond-haired girl." Earlier, during dinner, I had noticed that Mr. Herrera referred to Kate as *gata*, which Veronica said means "blue-eyed girl.")

"You heard her," J.P. put in. "Come have some fun. If you dare." He waggled his eyebrows at me.

I sighed. "Well, all right. Let's go."

I followed as Veronica and Jorge led the way through the back door. The moon was out, so it was pretty bright even though the sun had set. I hadn't been out that way yet, and I was surprised to see a big grove of palmlike trees stretching off behind the house. Veronica and Jorge explained that their family raised bananas on this piece of land, even though both her parents have office jobs. When I looked up at the tree I was passing, I recognized a clump of small greenish bananas growing way up at the top of the tall, skinny trunk just beneath the palmy leaves.

I didn't have much time to think about bananas, though. J.P. caught up to me and gave me a taunting smile as we all turned to follow Veronica and Jorge into the rain forest that stretched along the side of the banana trees. "Are you sure you're not scared, Bob?" So we were back to Bob again.

I rolled my eyes. Before I could say anything, there was a shriek from ahead. It was Jorge.

"Aaah! *Aaaahh-yiiiiiiii!*" he yelled loudly.

"What?" we all cried. "Jorge, what's wrong?" We rushed to see.

He was on the path leading into the rain forest, his eyes wide and his trembling finger pointing to something just off the path. "Eeeee!" he cried. "Look—a snake! I think it may be poisonous!"

I saw the snake right away. It was small and greenish brown, and it was starting to slither off into the underbrush. In the strong moonlight I recognized it right away from my research. It was a small tree boa, less than a foot long. That's a pretty common type of snake in Costa Rica, and it's perfectly harmless at that size since boas kill their prey by squeezing rather than by venom. I guessed that Jorge knew that too and was just trying to play a trick on us. I was sure of it when I glanced quickly at Veronica and saw that she was holding a hand over her mouth to hide a grin.

I looked around to see if anyone else was in on the joke, but Kate and Andy were backing away, looking worried. J.P. was standing his ground, but his smile had faded a little, so I guessed that he was scared too—though I was sure he would never admit it. Guys can be really ridiculous about stuff like that.

Then I had an idea. I decided I would handle this Jessica style.

I jumped forward. "I'll save you, Jorge!" I cried, pretending to be terrified but brave. I shoved my way past him and quickly reached down toward the snake. "Get away, you monster! Leave us alone!"

Behind me I could hear a loud gasp from Kate. "Elizabeth, be careful!" she shrieked. I felt kind of bad about tricking her, but I couldn't stop now.

I leaped up suddenly and sort of fell back toward the group. (By now the snake had disappeared into the thick underbrush that surrounded the path. Poor thing, I'm sure it was terrified by all the noise.)

"Aaaah!" I screamed loudly. "Help! I've been bitten! I feel woozy. I think I—" With that I slumped down onto the ground and pretended to pass out.

"Oh, no!" Kate squealed. "What should we do?"

"Don't panic!" J.P. said worriedly. "We have to—"

"Psych!" I cried suddenly, opening my eyes and jumping to my feet. "Gotcha!"

Veronica and Jorge started laughing hysterically. "Good one, Elizabeth!" Jorge said.

Veronica was almost doubled over, she was laughing so hard. "You are funny, Elizabeth!" she cried. "That was majorly cool!"

By now the others were laughing too. "You really had me going," Andy told me, still looking a bit nervous as he glanced at the spot where the snake had been.

"Me too," Kate exclaimed breathlessly.

J.P. hadn't said anything yet. When I glanced at him, he was giving me an admiring look. "What do you know," he said, shaking his head. "A practical joker."

I smiled, feeling as though I had scored a point or two in his eyes.

Then I had to go and ruin it. "For future reference," I said, looking at the other Americans, "you should know that that was a small, common type of tree boa. They're not poisonous, and they're probably more scared of you than you are of them."

"Wow!" Kate's eyes were wide and admiring. "How did you know that, Elizabeth?"

I shrugged. "I did my homework before I came,"

I said. "I checked out all the poisonous kinds of snakes so I'd be sure to recognize them if I ran into one."

"I did that too," Andy admitted. I noticed that he was blushing a little. "But I sort of panicked and forgot when I actually saw the snake."

I smiled at him reassuringly. "That could happen to anyone."

"Almost anyone," J.P. put in. His voice sounded odd, so I turned to look at him. He wasn't laughing anymore. "You would never make a mistake like that, would you, Elizabeth? You're always prepared."

What? I glanced at the others, who all looked as surprised as I felt.

"Yeah, I'm prepared," I said defensively. "Do you have a problem with that?"

There was a tense second. Then J.P. laughed. "No problem," he said lightly. "I'm just jealous because you're queen of the snakes and I'm not." He bowed low, scraping his hands on the ground in front of me. "All hail Queen Bob!"

The others laughed. I guessed they were relieved because he had avoided starting a real argument. I forced myself to laugh a little too. But I didn't feel very amused. Right then and there, I decided that enough was enough. For the rest of the time Jorge and Veronica were showing us around—pointing out more wildlife, explaining which plants and things were poisonous, even taking us to peek at Gemelo, which was only about a ten-minute walk through the forest—I stuck close to Kate and Andy and avoided talking to J.P. at all.

I've decided I'm going to do that as much as possible from now on. I may have to work with J.P., but that doesn't mean we have to be friends, especially if he's so determined to make fun of me every chance he gets.

*Sunday, 10:10 p.m.*

I still can't believe what happened at lunchtime today. For most of this morning I thought things were going really smoothly. But it was just the calm before the storm.

As we started to work, a few of the kids complained about the heat, which was worse than usual today, but most of them worked really hard. J.P. was cracking jokes the whole time, of course, including quite a few at my expense. He had gotten tired of calling me Madame Foreman and had shortened it to Madame Bob.

I did my best to ignore him.

By the time we broke for lunch, I was feeling pretty good. We had gotten even more done than I'd hoped, and I estimated we would be finished with the framing by Thursday afternoon at the latest. I remember hoping that the supply truck would arrive soon, maybe even today, so we wouldn't lose any time.

The villagers had set up a long table in a shady

area behind the construction site, where we eat lunch each day as a group. A few of the villagers brought out our food and drinks and then left us to our meal. The food was delicious as always, and it was pleasant sitting there beneath the trees, listening to the monkeys chattering and the birds calling in the forest. I was sitting with Kate and Andy and Sumi and Will, talking about what we had to do that afternoon.

We had been eating for a while when Veronica wandered out of her house with her little sister, Eugenia. The two of them came over to say hi and see how we were doing. I told her how much we'd gotten done already, feeling proud of our hard work.

"Cool," Veronica said. "Why don't you reward yourselves and come hang out in the forest with us? There's lots more to see in the daytime."

"Sorry," I said, smiling at her eagerness. "We got a lot done, but there's a lot more to do. We have to keep working."

J.P. was sitting a few seats down, but I guess he'd been listening, because he leaned over. "Come on, Madame Bob," he called. "Don't be such a slave driver. Let's have some fun. After all, we're finished with the foundation."

I shot him an annoyed look. "Not quite," I reminded him.

He shrugged and looked around the table. The other kids on the crew were listening by now, and some of them were whispering to each other.

"Please, 'Lizabeta?" Eugenia pleaded. "We want have fun!" (She doesn't speak English quite as well as the older kids.)

"Please, 'Lizabeta?" J.P. grinned and imitated the little girl. He clasped his hands in front of him. "We worked hard all morning. Don't we deserve a break?"

"But if we keep working, we have a chance to get ahead of schedule," I pointed out.

"Is that supposed to convince us?" J.P. rolled his eyes. "And hey, don't the words *summer vacation* mean anything to you?" A few other kids mumbled agreement.

Andy jumped to my defense. "Come on, guys," he said. "Elizabeth's right. We should keep working. Maybe we can be finished with the framing by the time that supply truck gets here."

"But here in Costa Rica schedules are often late," Veronica spoke up. "The truck might not arrive for a week yet or even more. And why should you all waste an awesome day like today when it could start pouring dogs and cats tomorrow?"

J.P. pushed back his empty plate and stared at me with that challenging look in his eye. "Come on, boss lady," he taunted. "You heard Veronica, and she should know. She lives here. Now are you going to let us go? Or do we all have detention?"

I bit my lip, feeling trapped. Once I thought about it, I could see why they wanted to go explore.

Still, it was only our third day of work. We had a responsibility to do our job—that was why we had signed up for this trip. I had to forbid J.P. and the others to go. It was the right thing to do.

But I was scared. What would happen if I said no and they went anyway?

Sometimes being a leader stinks.

Before I could decide what to do, little Eugenia let out an excited squeal. *"Mira!"* she cried. "Big bird!" She was pointing to a huge, brightly colored parrot perched on the roof of a nearby building. I recognized it from my research as a scarlet macaw.

As we all turned to see, the bird let out a raucous caw and flew off, heading for the thick rain forest on the far side of the construction site. Eugenia was already running after it, with Veronica right behind her. Before I realized what was happening, most of the other kids had hopped up and were racing after them, shouting and laughing as they tried to catch up to the beautiful parrot. Even Kate got caught up in the excitement. Within seconds almost everyone had disappeared into the rain forest. Only Andy and I were left sitting at the table.

Andy stared after the others, looking shocked. "I can't believe they just ran off like that," he exclaimed. "They'd better come back so we can get back to work."

"I don't think we should hold our breath," I told him. I could already guess what was going to happen.

Once the other kids were out there in the rain forest having fun, they weren't going to want to return, especially if they believed they had earned some free time. And unless I missed my guess, J.P. would talk them all into believing exactly that. Hadn't he almost convinced me just now?

Andy was shaking his head. "Now I can see why Marion wanted you to be foreman," he said. "You're the only one here with a sense of responsibility."

For some reason Andy's words made me feel even worse. In fact, I felt like I might start crying Not only had the other kids totally ignored me, but now they were all off having fun while I was stuck here—left out. Had I made a mistake by not letting them go in the first place?

The rest of the afternoon was miserable. Andy followed me around like a puppy dog, hanging on my every word and staring at me constantly. After a couple of hours I was ready to strangle him.

Not that he's not a really nice guy, of course. He's smart and well read, and he wouldn't be bad looking if he'd fix his hair and maybe get more attractive frames for his glasses. Actually, he'd be kind of cute. But there's no way I would ever be interested in him. Anyway, today I really wished he would leave me alone so I could feel sorry for myself in private. This had been my chance to be a cool foreman, and I had blown it.

The others got back right before it was time to
head back to the main village for dinner. They
came running into the clearing with J.P. in the lead
just as Andy and I were putting away our tools.
They all seemed breathless and happy. Even Loren
was actually smiling.

"Yo! Bob!" J.P. cried when he spotted me. "We're
back. Did you miss us?"

I scowled at him and didn't answer.

Andy stepped forward. "It wasn't very nice of
you guys to run off like that," he said. "Elizabeth
was being a responsible foreman, and it was really
rude to ignore her."

Kate bit her lip guiltily. "Oh, no," she said. "I
didn't think about that, Elizabeth. I'm sorry."

"I'm sorry, too, *macha*," Veronica said quickly, hurrying over and putting her arm around my shoulders. "We weren't trying to dis you. But you should
have come with us. We had so much awesome fun!"

"Yeah," put in a girl named Anne. "Veronica
showed us all sorts of cool stuff in the rain forest.
We saw a river and waterfall . . ."

". . . and a lot of interesting birds and animals,"
Sumi said.

Kate nodded, her eyes shining. "I saw more parrots and some monkeys, and I even spotted a sloth
hanging upside down way up high in a tree."

"It was cool," Loren added. Now I knew they'd
had a great time. I'd never heard her say so many
words at once.

They continued to describe their day, not seeming to notice that it was making me feel horrible. Obviously I had missed an amazing time. And for what? It wasn't as though Andy and I had gotten a ton of work done by ourselves. In fact, we hadn't been able to do much work at all without the others' help. That had given me plenty of time to feel sorry for myself and Andy plenty of time to stare at me. But it hadn't done much in the way of getting the community center built.

Oh, well. Who needs fun on their summer vacation anyway?

*MONDAY, 9:35 P.M.*

When I got to the site this morning, I prepared myself for more taunting remarks from J.P. about what happened yesterday. Kate and Veronica had spent all evening apologizing (whenever Veronica's parents and grandmother weren't listening, that is). But I was sure that J.P. wasn't feeling sorry about the adventure at all. He'd probably spent all night concocting more new and humiliating jokes at my expense.

But nobody even looked up as Kate and I arrived. Kate wandered off as I went to unlock the office shack, and soon she and Andy were arguing over some obscure species of plant they had spotted by the side of the house yesterday. Tiffany was giggling as Will and Ricky tried to speak Spanish.

Loren was listening as Ty talked about baseball. Sumi, Anne, and Bridget were chatting about school.

Only J.P. was being quiet. That was pretty unusual for him. And I quickly noticed that whenever he looked my way, a new expression came over his face. Not amusement, not mischievousness, not unfriendliness . . . I couldn't figure it out at first. It took me a while to recognize it.

It was pity.

As soon as it dawned on me I felt more horrible than ever. J.P. wasn't bothering to tease me anymore because he actually felt sorry for me. After all, I had proved I was a dork in front of everyone.

It was humiliating. And I wasn't sure how to react.

I kept trying to figure out a way to show J.P. that I wasn't the totally lame, boring person he thought I was. Then I kept trying to figure out why I cared what he thought. My thoughts went around and around, circling between those two points. And finally the truth dawned on me.

I didn't want J.P. to stop teasing me.

I definitely didn't want him to think I was a dork.

I . . . liked him.

As in *crushville*.

I tried to come up with another explanation, but there was none. How could I actually *like* him when he drives me *nuts?*

For the first time I understood how Jessica feels when she's trying to impress some jerk like Bruce Patman. Well, maybe not Bruce. He's way more obnoxious than J.P. could ever hope to be. Meaner and snobbier too. But you know what I mean.

Thinking of Jessica made me feel homesick. I guess maybe that sounds kind of babyish. But Jessica is always a really good person to talk to—especially about guy problems. She would probably know exactly what I should do about J.P.

So basically it's hopeless. I've finally discovered that I like J.P.—at the exact same moment he's decided I'm a loser. And we're stuck together for the next four weeks!

# *Five*

◇

I just read over what I wrote on Monday, and I guess I was feeling pretty down. But a lot can change in a day or two!

The thing with J.P. was bugging me all day yesterday. I didn't want his pity. I didn't want him to think I was a total loser.

It was all I could think about all day, and by evening it was driving me berserk!

I decided I had to talk to him. So after dinner I went next door to find him. He wasn't there, but Andy was. He told me J.P. had gone off to try to spot bats in the rain forest. Andy looked kind of disappointed that I had come over looking for J.P. and not for him, but I didn't have time to deal with that just then.

I went out into the forest. It didn't take me long to find J.P. because he was singing the theme song from that old TV show *Batman* at the top of his lungs. I could have told him that wasn't a very good way to spot wildlife, but I figured I'd better avoid saying anything that made me sound like an even bigger dork.

He looked surprised to see me. "Oh, hello, Elizabeth," he said. "Out here looking for your library card?"

I bit my lip. I couldn't believe it, but I actually missed hearing him call me Bob. "Ha-ha," I said weakly. "Actually, I was looking for you."

"What's up?" That pitying look was back.

"I think—," I began, but I didn't get any further because I heard someone calling my name. It was Andy. I pressed my lips together to keep from screaming with frustration as he raced over to us, breathless and red faced. He was running so fast, he tripped over a big tree root and almost went flying flat on his face. J.P. jumped forward just in time and caught him.

"Thanks," Andy gasped once he was upright again.

"No problem, man," J.P. replied. "Were you looking for our fearless leader? Here she is." He waved a hand in my direction.

I was annoyed at Andy. He knew I had come out here looking for J.P. So why was he butting in?

Andy didn't notice me glaring at him, though.

He was really worked up about something. "Listen, I just heard some big news," he exclaimed. "I—I—it—"

He was so overwrought that he was sort of sputtering, having trouble getting the words out. J.P. reached over and thumped him on the back.

"Spit it out, Andy!" he cried. "Before you choke."

Andy nodded, took a deep breath, and started speaking again more slowly. "One of the local kids just told me," he said. "He said the supply truck got to Gemelo this afternoon right after lunch."

I frowned, not understanding. What Andy was saying didn't make sense. "But that can't be true. Gemelo is only a quarter of a mile away," I said. "If the truck had been there then, it should have been to our village just a short while after that."

Andy was already waving his hands around. "I know," he said. "But listen, that's what I'm trying to tell you! The truck was going to come here next. But while it was in Gemelo, Tanya stole the gas cap and hid it!"

"What?" I gasped. "Why would she do that?"

But even as I said it, I already knew the answer. Tanya wanted to win that Outstanding Volunteer award at the end of the trip. She wanted it a *lot*. So she decided to deliberately delay the supply truck. If it was stuck in her village, our village wouldn't get our supplies on time. That would give her crew a big head start on their building and make her look like a great leader.

As I was thinking all that, Andy was saying approximately the same thing. He's pretty smart. He had figured it out right away too, even though he said none of the adults had any idea what had happened to the gas cap.

J.P. caught on quickly. His grin faded and was replaced with a grim expression. "Yeah," he said. "That sounds like Tanya."

"It's not fair." I was furious. We were supposed to be here to help these people, not to get into some big competition over winning the Outstanding Volunteer plaque.

My first instinct was to get in touch with Robert and Marion and tell them. But the thought of that made me uncomfortable for a couple of reasons. For one, some people (J.P. for instance) might think I'm kind of a goody-goody, but I've never been the kind of person who tells on others. Besides that, we really didn't have any proof about what Tanya had done. I had no trouble believing it, but an adult would probably want to give her the benefit of the doubt.

No, we had to take care of this ourselves. At first I considered going over to Gemelo and confronting Tanya. If I reminded her why we were really here, maybe she would see how selfish she was being and return the gas cap. I don't know, appealing to Tanya's softer side didn't seem *too* likely to work, but maybe it was worth a shot.

I was getting ready to tell the two guys that idea.

But suddenly out of nowhere another idea popped into my head. A daring idea. A sneaky idea.

Another very Jessica-like idea!

"Listen," I said casually. "I think we can handle this on our own."

"But shouldn't we tell someone?" Andy said anxiously. "If we don't get our supplies soon—"

"Don't worry about it," I interrupted. The idea was turning itself over and over in my mind. It would be risky, yes. But I could do it. The details were already coming into focus. "Have you told anyone else what you heard?"

Andy shook his head. "I came straight out to find you."

"Good." I glanced at J.P., who was staring at me curiously. "You'll keep quiet too, right?"

He shrugged. "Sure, no problem."

He didn't say anything more, but I could see that he was wondering what I was up to. I'm sure he figured I was planning to run straight to Robert and Marion. Boy, was he ever wrong.

I spent the next few hours planning my scheme. The only detail that worried me was finding another snake, especially in the dark. I borrowed a flashlight from Jorge, then hid out in my room, pretending to sleep, until the house fell silent.

I decided I might as well start looking in the same spot where Jorge had found the young tree boa. I snuck out of the house, tiptoed through the banana grove, and headed into the rain forest.

After a few minutes of shining the flashlight around in the underbrush, I spotted a small boa similar to the one we'd seen before. I got as close as I could before making my move—I didn't want to make a mistake and grab a poisonous viper! I managed to grab it, picking it up by the neck just behind the head as I'd seen people do on TV, though it did its best to wriggle out of my grasp and slither away.

"Sorry, little snake," I whispered. "I need your help." I tucked it into the pocket of the Windbreaker I was wearing and zipped the pocket shut. The snake wiggled around a bit, then seemed to accept its fate and settled down.

I grinned as I headed for the path to Gemelo, trying to imagine what Jessica would say if she could see me now. She hates snakes. She thinks they're gross and slimy, no matter how many times I tell her that their skin is actually smooth and sort of rubbery. She wouldn't touch a snake if someone paid her a million dollars. At least that's what she claims. Personally, I think if it came right down to it, she'd *kiss* a snake if someone paid her a million dollars to do it.

Not that I intended to kiss this particular snake. But I did have big plans for it.

I hurried along the path to Gemelo, listening to the night sounds all around me. I had read about how a lot of creatures in the rain forest are more active after dark, and that seemed to be true. It was amazing how many different calls, whistles, shrieks, croaks, and so on I heard during that ten-minute walk. It was kind of scary, actually, even though there was a bright full moon and I had my flashlight.

Still, I knew I wasn't in any real danger as long as I stayed on the trail, which was wide and easy to follow. The only big meat-eating animals in the Costa Rican forests are jaguars, and I'd read that they're afraid of humans and hardly ever seen near villages. And I knew how to recognize the most common poisonous snakes—ten-foot bushmasters, six-foot yellow beard vipers, and smaller, but still deadly eyelash vipers—so I could steer well clear of them. Not that they were likely to bite me through my jeans and heavy boots.

Soon I was at the outskirts of Gemelo. The tents where the student volunteers were sleeping were off to the right. I stuck my flashlight in the pocket that didn't have the snake in it and crept along just inside the screen of trees until I reached the camp. Now all I had to do was find Tanya's tent.

I got very lucky. All the tents had little name tags stuck to the front of them, and Tanya's tent was at the edge of the group, close to where I was standing. I spotted it right away.

I spent a few more minutes getting the lay of the land and figuring out my exact moves. The tent was about six feet long and four feet wide, with zippered entrances at the front and back. There were also a couple of windows, but they were zipped shut as well, so I couldn't see in. That meant I couldn't check to make sure Tanya was sleeping. But I figured that by this time of night, it was a pretty safe bet.

When I was sure I had figured out the best way to carry out my plan, I took a deep breath. My heart was beating fast. Was this really me, Elizabeth Wakefield, the responsible, smart, serious girl everyone knew? Was I really going to do something so sneaky, and risky, and crazy—without any prompting or pleading from Jessica at all? Usually she's the only one who can talk me into doing daring things.

But now, here I had gone and talked myself into it!

I decided not to put it off any longer or I would lose my nerve. I unzipped my jacket pocket and grabbed the snake. It seemed kind of annoyed—I think it must have gone to sleep in my nice, warm pocket while I was walking.

"Here goes nothing," I whispered to it. Then I crept forward as quietly as I could to the back of Tanya's tent.

Holding my breath, I unzipped the rear door a few inches. Then I crouched down and peered in.

It was dark in the tent, and it took my eyes a few seconds to adjust. I could hear the sound of deep breathing, but it took a moment before I was able to pick out the shadowy blob lying just a foot in front of me. It was Tanya, and she was obviously fast asleep. It was warm in the tent, and she had pushed the top part of her sleeping bag halfway down her body. *Perfect!* I thought.

Now that the moment was here, I wasn't nervous at all. I reached forward silently, the wriggling snake in my hand. Nudging the sleeping bag back a little farther to create an opening, I sort of tossed the boa as best I could into the warm, dark depths of the sleeping bag. I quickly scooted back and rezipped the tent door. Then I moved aside and held my breath, waiting.

I didn't have to wait long. After a few seconds I heard some shuffling sounds from the other side of the tent wall. That was quickly followed by an ear-shattering scream.

"Bingo," I whispered to myself, grinning.

A second later I heard Tanya scrabbling at the front of the tent, then quickly unzipping the door. At the same time, even over her continuing screams, came the sounds of people stirring in the surrounding tents.

"What's going on out there?" a male voice shouted from a nearby tent.

*"Qué ruido!"* someone cried from over toward the houses.

"Help! Help!" Tanya wailed at the top of her lungs.

I knew I had to act fast. Soon Tanya's piercing shrieks would have the entire village wide awake.

I unzipped the back of the tent just enough to scoot through. Whipping out my flashlight and covering it with my hand so it wouldn't show through the tent wall, I began my search. I figured I had five minutes at the most before Tanya returned with a snake-hunting posse.

There wasn't much in the tent. Just the sleeping bag, one large suitcase, and a small leather backpack. I decided to check the backpack first. I opened the main compartment and searched through the contents. The gas cap wasn't there, but something else was—a very familiar-looking white plastic bag.

I gasped and yanked it out to look inside. Sure enough, it was full of rock CDs and movie magazines. It was the going-away present from Jessica! I didn't stop to think much about it at that moment—just shoved it under my jacket and kept searching—but obviously Tanya must have overheard Jess and me at the airport, then later saw me sneaking back to leave the bag for the Canadian girls. And she decided to pick it up and keep it for herself.

But as I said, I didn't have much time to think about it then. I could still hear Tanya's screams somewhere in the distance, along with a growing number of other voices. I continued my search and soon found what I was looking for in one of the backpack's outside pockets. The gas cap was wrapped in some paper towels and shoved way down to the bottom. I stuck it in my jacket pocket and zipped it in safely.

Then I paused. I couldn't leave that poor, innocent little snake in the tent. Crawling toward the back entrance, I paused at the sleeping bag. I unzipped its whole length, but the small boa was nowhere to be seen.

I glanced around worriedly. Where had it gone? I started to search the corners of the tent, but just then the chorus of loud voices seemed to get louder—as if they were heading in my direction.

*Uh-oh. Tanya's coming back with reinforcements,* I thought. *Sorry, snake,* I added reluctantly. *You're on your own.* I hoped it had escaped through the open front or back flaps while I was searching. I quickly escaped out the back flap myself, zipping it behind me. Seconds later I was back in the rain forest, safely hidden from the people who were now streaming toward Tanya's tent. Tanya herself was in the lead, a grim expression on her face and her prissy lace-trimmed nightgown waving in the breeze.

I grinned. I'd done it! But I didn't stick around to gloat. I didn't want to risk being spotted. I hurried through the trees to the place where the main road entered the village. The supply truck was parked there, dark and silent. The gas tank was on the side closest to the forest, so I was able to quickly dart out and screw the gas cap back on without being seen. Once that was done, I hurried back to the trail and raced toward home, laughing to myself all the way.

About halfway here I realized something. I had known that my plan was necessary because it was the best way to ruin Tanya's evil plan. But now I saw that it had been more than that.

It had been fun! In fact, it was by far the most fun I'd had since the trip began. Maybe the most fun I'd had all year!

Hmmm. Did that mean Jessica had been right all these years? Something to think about. . . .

Anyway, it turned out that the snake hadn't escaped after all. Because Robert and Marion stopped by our village the next morning to talk to us.

They gathered us all in the main clearing again. "Something happened in Gemelo last night," Robert began abruptly, staring around at all of us. "Someone played a prank on Tanya, the team leader over there, and we want to know if anyone here had anything to do with it."

"What kind of prank?" J.P. called out.

Robert shot him a suspicious look and said nothing. But Marion spoke up. "Well, we're actually not completely sure it was a prank. But somehow a snake got into Tanya's tent even though she claims it was zipped closed. It found its way into her sleeping bag."

There was some laughter at that, as well as some horrified gasps. I guess people's reactions depended on how they felt about snakes—and about Tanya.

"It's not funny," Robert said sternly. "This could have been a very serious incident if she had been bitten."

"Luckily the snake wasn't poisonous," Marion added quickly and soothingly. "One of the village boys was among the people who helped her search for the snake, and he recognized it. It was just a small, common type of tree boa, quite shy and harmless. They released it back into the forest."

I was busy pretending to be as shocked about this whole story as everyone else. But out of the corner of my eye I noticed J.P. turn to look at me when Marion mentioned the kind of snake. He was giving me an odd look.

I grinned briefly in return, then turned away. I wondered if he had guessed my secret. He knew I had some kind of plan to get back at Tanya. And he knew I could tell the difference between a poisonous snake and an ordinary one.

I hadn't thought about it when I came up with my plan, but now I wondered. Would this help convince him I wasn't so dull after all?

Marion and Robert said a few more words about how we shouldn't think of this as a competition, how pranks can sometimes be mean or dangerous, etc. They also said that as soon as the gas cap was found, the supply truck would be on its way, so we should work hard so we would be ready.

I could hardly stop myself from smiling when they said that. I had a strong feeling the gas cap would be discovered very soon. And I could only imagine what everyone would say when they saw that it was right back on the truck where it belonged.

Elizabeth Wakefield, you are a genius!

# Six

THURSDAY, 9:25 P.M.

Earlier today I had a great idea about what to do with the bag of stuff I'd taken back from Tanya. When I grabbed it, I just sort of thought that she shouldn't have it because it wasn't hers. But I still didn't want it either.

Then I realized who would really appreciate it. Veronica! I knew it wasn't easy for her to get the kind of stuff that was in that bag, and I was sure she would love it.

I didn't want anyone else to see me give it to her, though. For one thing, I didn't want anyone to think I had ignored instructions and brought the stuff with me. More important, if Tanya had shown it to anyone (which I seriously doubted, but you never know), I would be busted.

So I waited for a chance to talk to Veronica alone. Everyone was around at breakfast, and it was Veronica's turn to help her parents clean up afterward, so I couldn't say anything then. I made sure the plastic bag was stuffed deep down in my suitcase, then headed for the construction site.

The supplies still weren't there, of course, but we still had almost a full day's work to do on the framing. So we all set to work right after breakfast.

We worked hard all morning, and I was feeling pretty good about it. Somehow my sneaky trick on Tanya had made me feel more confident about being foreman, even though nobody else knew about it. Well, except maybe J.P. He still didn't say much to me, but that pitying look was gone, and he kept glancing at me curiously when he thought I wasn't looking.

We broke for lunch and then got back to work. Veronica wandered by a little while later to say hi. Seeing my chance, I pulled her aside and quickly whispered that I had a surprise for her after work.

"You must spill your guts immediately, Elizabeth," she squealed. "Otherwise I will die! I will totally die!"

"Ssh!" I hushed her, looking around nervously. If she kept this up, someone would hear. "I can't tell you in front of everyone. It's a secret."

That only made things worse. "Ooh! I love secrets!" Veronica exclaimed. "Please, please, please tell me now, OK? We can sneak into the forest where nobody will hear."

I should have known she'd react that way. After all, she reminds me so much of Jessica—and since when could Jess ever wait even two seconds to hear a juicy secret? I was about to insist that we wait until my crew finished for the day. That would only be a few hours from now, and I didn't think it would be right to leave even for a few minutes. There were more than enough people to finish the framing, but the supply truck might arrive at any time.

Then I stopped to think about that. Who knew how long it would take someone to notice that the gas cap had been returned? Besides, after all the rains and flooding, a lot of the roads around here were in pretty bad shape. It might still take a long time for the truck to get here, and then I would have stayed for nothing.

I didn't want to miss any more chances for fun. Not after what had happened the other day. After all, why should I feel guilty about leaving my crew for a few minutes? Hadn't they all run off without a second thought for me just a few days earlier? I deserved some time off too. They owed it to me. Didn't they?

I was a little bit uncomfortable with that line of thought. It sounded kind of selfish. But hadn't it been selfish of them to ignore me and run off chasing a parrot all afternoon?

I had to stop worrying about it. *Go for it, Lizzie!* I told myself, just like Jessica would do. Then I grinned at Veronica. "Go distract everyone for a second," I whispered. "I'll sneak away and meet you in the banana grove in ten minutes."

Veronica giggled with delight. Then she winked and strolled away.

I continued to work. A moment later I heard Veronica shriek loudly from the other side of the site. "Ow!" she cried. "Somebody help me. I think I stepped on a nail!"

For a second I nearly threw down my tools and rushed to help her. Then I realized that this was her distraction. So while everyone else hurried toward Veronica, I hurried in the opposite direction— toward the Herreras' house.

I knew Mr. and Mrs. Herrera were working today, and the little kids and their grandmother were spending the day with some friends in Gemelo. So I didn't have to be quiet as I rushed inside and grabbed the white plastic bag out of my suitcase.

I hurried to the meeting spot and waited for Veronica to show up. When she arrived, laughing breathlessly, we raced away into the forest.

"Follow me, *macha*," Veronica said. "I know the most awesome place to go."

Ten minutes later we emerged in a beautiful little clearing. "Oh, Veronica!" I exclaimed. "It really *is* awesome!" I looked around at the mossy, shaded ground, the rapidly tumbling stream that cut the clearing in half, and the tropical birds flitting around the edges of the clearing in the tall trees of the rain forest canopy. It was positively gorgeous.

She grinned. "Jorge and I come here often with our friends," she explained, sitting down cross-legged on the bank of the stream. She pointed at the water. "We call this stream Río Risa, which means 'river of laughter,' because the water sounds like it's always giggling. It joins up with a large river just a short distance away."

"It's wonderful," I told her. "I'm so glad you brought me here. And now . . ." I reached for the bag.

Needless to say, Veronica loved my gift. She was practically in heaven as she pulled out each CD and magazine. Her family doesn't have a CD player, but her neighbors (the ones J.P. and Andy are staying with) have one, and there's also that portable one in the office shack, which she's sure Marion will let her borrow sometime. I made her promise not to show her new things to anyone—not even Jorge—until after the five weeks were up. I didn't want anyone to find out I stole them from Tanya, even if they had been mine to begin with.

Anyway, I guess after that I kind of forgot about going back to work. Veronica and I were having so much fun, talking and laughing and getting to know each other better.

I was telling Veronica all about one of Jessica's crazy ideas when a loud voice interrupted me. "So this is where you've been hiding out all day!"

I whirled around with a gasp, fearing that Robert and Marion had somehow discovered I was missing and tracked me down. But it wasn't them. It was J.P. And he was grinning.

Suddenly feeling nervous, I stared back at him. He looked incredibly cute in his cargo shorts and pocket T-shirt. For about the millionth time I wondered what he really thought of me.

I gulped. "Uh, we were just heading back to the village," I said quickly.

But Veronica and Jessica turned out to have even more in common than I thought. Not only did Veronica somehow sense what was going on, but she decided to do something about it. "Don't worry about walking me back, *macha*," she said. "I must go now anyway to help Mamá prepare dinner. You might as well stay here with J.P."

Before I could respond, Veronica tossed me a quick wink, then took off at top speed. A second later she had disappeared into the forest.

I grinned weakly at J.P., shifting my weight from foot to foot and feeling more nervous than ever now that we were alone. But I was also feeling something else. I guess you'd call it anticipation. This was it—it was my chance to find out how things stood between us. If there was anything between us at all.

J.P. spoke first. "So, Bob," he said casually. "I was just thinking about that snake they found in

Tanya's tent night before last. I wonder who could have put it there?"

I couldn't help it—my heart gave a little involuntary leap when he called me Bob. And it was obvious that he'd figured out I'd been responsible for Tanya's snake. I gave what I hoped was a casual shrug. "Who knows?" I said, trying to imitate the coy tone of voice Jess uses when she's teasing a guy she likes. I wasn't about to give him the satisfaction of being right too quickly. "I have no idea how it could have gotten there."

"Hmmm." J.P. stroked his chin thoughtfully. "Are you sure you don't know anything about it?" He took a step or two closer until he was standing just a couple of feet away. He raised one eyebrow and wriggled it quizzically.

He looked so silly that I couldn't help giggling. "Nope," I replied. I had to tilt my head back a little to look him in the face since he was a few inches taller than me. "I have no idea. Maybe it just slithered in there by itself." I giggled again. "It could have used its tail to unzip the door."

J.P. laughed. "Maybe," he agreed. "Or maybe somebody here is keeping secrets."

"Maybe," I said mysteriously. "So what are we going to do about it?" I don't mind saying I was feeling pretty pleased with myself. *So this is what flirting is all about!* I thought. Whenever I'd tried to flirt with a guy I liked in the past, like Todd, I'd usually ended up feeling pretty stupid and awkward. But this was different. This was fun!

"Well, I could ask my witness," J.P. said.

For a split second I started to panic. Had someone seen me that night?

Then I saw that he was pointing to the front pocket of his T-shirt. Now that I looked closer, I saw a bulge there. "I found the accomplice behind the banana grove this morning," he said. "Now are you going to tell me what happened, or do I have to ask the little guy here?" He patted the bulge gently.

"You can't trick me that easily," I retorted. "I know you don't speak Snake."

"Curses. Foiled again." J.P. pretended to think hard for a second, putting a finger to his chin and frowning. "Well, then," he said at last. "As I see it, there's just one solution. We'll have to play truth or dare." He gave me one of his challenging grins. "If you dare, that is."

"I dare," I said quickly. "You can even go first if you want."

"Good." He put his hands on his hips. "Elizabeth Bob Wakefield, truth or dare?"

For a second I was tempted to say dare, just to see what he would come up with for me to do. But I changed my mind. I was feeling bolder but not quite that brave. "Truth," I said firmly.

"OK." He grinned. "Here's your question. Did you put that snake in Tanya's tent night before last?"

Rules are rules, right? I knew I had to answer truthfully. "Yes," I said. "I did."

"Aha!" he crowed. "I knew it. So why did you do it? Simple revenge?"

I was trying to figure out how to answer. But just then I noticed movement in J.P.'s shirt pocket. A second later the snake inside stuck its head out into the air, flicked its tongue once or twice, and started to slither up toward his shoulder.

My heart stopped. I swear it did. Because it wasn't another tree boa—it was an eyelash viper. And it was poisonous!

Later, once I thought about it, I saw how he could have made that mistake, especially if he'd found the snake near the same spot where we'd seen the other one. It was about the same size as the young boa, and the coloring was sort of similar, though the viper had a faint diamond pattern on its back. But it also had one very important distinguishing feature that helped me recognize it so fast—a sort of visor-shaped thing over its eyes, which is what gave it its name.

I was horrified when I saw that snake crawling out of J.P.'s pocket. I knew from my research that several people die each year in Costa Rica from being bitten by eyelash vipers. He was incredibly lucky that it hadn't bitten him when he picked it up! But now it was winding its way straight toward J.P.'s face. . . .

"Hold still!" I shouted. At the same time I

leaped forward and knocked the snake off to the side, sending it flying onto the ground a few feet away. It lay there stunned for a second before slithering off into the underbrush.

J.P. looked a bit stunned too. "Hey, what did you do that for, Bob?" he demanded, sounding indignant. "I was going to keep him as a pet while we're here."

Now that it was over, I felt a bit woozy. I collapsed onto a nearby fallen log (after checking to make sure there were no snakes on it). I knew we had both been lucky. That snake could have bitten J.P. through his shirt before I ever saw it, and it could have bitten me on the hand when I knocked it off. I didn't like to think about what might have happened next.

J.P. was still staring at me, waiting for an explanation.

"That—that wasn't the same kind of snake," I explained shakily. "It wasn't a boa at all. It was a viper—a poisonous one. Really poisonous."

J.P.'s face turned pale. "You're not kidding me, are you?" he asked softly.

I shook my head. And I guess he could tell from my face that I meant it because he plopped down on the log next to me.

"Wow," he said flatly. "Wow." I could tell he was realizing just how close he had come to getting bitten.

He turned and gave me a serious look. I was still

feeling shaky, but I also couldn't help noticing how close together we were sitting. When he faced me, I was looking straight into his hazel eyes.

"Thanks, Elizabeth," he said. "That was a close one. From now on I'm not going to touch anything else in this place without checking with you first."

I smiled weakly. "Good."

He smiled back. "In fact, I'm going to stick to you like glue from now on. You don't mind, do you?"

"No."

That was all I could say. Because my heart had stopped again. This time it was because his face was moving closer. Then closer still. His eyes were locked on mine. I felt myself leaning forward a little bit in response to the look he was giving me. Was he going to kiss me? His gaze was pulling me toward him like a magnet. Closer . . . closer . . .

I closed my eyes, anticipating fireworks, but instead I got—shouts. Faint shouts coming from the direction of the village.

We pulled apart at the same time. "What was that?" I asked, but I was thinking, *Drat, drat, drat!* Just like that—our romantic moment was ruined. The Kiss That Never Was.

He shook his head. "Sounds like something big," he commented with a little frown.

But now that we had pulled apart, my senses were coming back to me. Maybe someone had noticed we were missing. Maybe they were heading this way, searching for us. I didn't want anyone to catch us like this.

"Come on," I said reluctantly. "I guess we should see what's going on."

He nodded and climbed to his feet, reaching down a hand to help me up. He stepped aside to let me go down the path first, putting one hand on my back to guide me along. Then he dropped his hand again, and we walked along almost as if nothing had happened. Which it hadn't, not really.

But I knew something *had* happened. Something special. I wasn't sure I understood it, but maybe that didn't matter. I did my best not to let my grin of pure happiness break out into laughter as we walked toward the village. Now I was really glad I had gone off with Veronica earlier. I was even glad J.P. had grabbed the wrong snake. Otherwise this wonderful moment might never have happened!

We got our first glimpse of the construction site through a thick screen of tree branches and hibiscus bushes. Even so, we saw right away what was going on. The supply truck had arrived. When I saw it, I felt like kicking myself. If only I'd let Tanya keep the stupid gas cap, J.P. and I could have hung out in that clearing all afternoon!

That gave me an idea. Another very wicked, Jessica-like idea. Once upon a time I would have ignored it. But since starting this trip, I've realized that those wicked, Jessica-like ideas can sometimes be the very best ideas of all.

"Come on." I grabbed J.P.'s hand and dragged him back farther into the trees before anyone spotted us.

He looked surprised. I noticed he didn't drop my hand, though. "What is it?"

I grinned. "Nobody knows where we are, right? And there are plenty of people around to unload the supplies from the truck."

"Yeah." J.P.'s eyes were already starting to sparkle. "So?"

I shrugged. "It's going to be dinnertime soon. We won't be able to start doing any serious building today. So what's our hurry to get back?"

"I'm in no hurry," he said smiling down at me. "Besides, I still have a few things to ask you about your trip to Tanya's tent. We'd better go discuss it back in that clearing."

I quickly turned and headed back. I knew he was just joking around, but I didn't want him to ask me again about why I had planted the snake. I wasn't sure how I should answer that question.

Somehow I didn't think J.P. would approve of the main reason, which was to get the gas cap back so we could get started on our building. He might think I was being competitive, like Tanya herself, instead of fun loving and daring. And I liked having him think I was fun loving and daring. Actually, I was feeling pretty fun loving and daring just then. Anyway, I didn't want to actually lie to J.P., but I figured that if we never got around to discussing my little trip to Tanya's village again, there would never be any reason to share the whole truth.

"I'm right behind you, Elizabeth," he said.

I smiled. *What a bonus*, I thought. *Not only is this turning out to be the most wonderful afternoon of my life—but J.P. has finally stopped calling me Bob!*

# Seven

When we got to the site this morning, we found that the local builder had shown up. His name is José and he can't be much more than sixteen or seventeen years old. And he's absolutely gorgeous. At least that's what Veronica says. As soon as she laid eyes on him, she was head over heels in love. She's been hanging around the site all morning, helping with the work. Especially any work that José happens to be involved in.

Actually, Veronica kept trying to get me to come help her flirt with José. But I wasn't much help. José is so serious that he didn't seem to notice us at all except as part of his group of workers. He just kept ordering us to do different tasks, hardly giving us a second to take a breath let alone try to flirt with him or even talk to each other.

While I was busy counting nails and sawing two-by-fours, I kept thinking that there had to be a way to make this more fun. I knew I had started out wanting to work as hard as I could, but that just didn't seem to be enough anymore. Whenever I glanced over at J.P., I saw him working away diligently. I guess it was because he'd had so much fun hanging yesterday (he never did kiss me, by the way, but we still had a great time), so now he could throw himself into his tasks with extra energy. It was sort of like the way the others had settled down to work after taking that day off last Sunday.

But that enthusiasm would be sure to fade quickly if we didn't get to have more fun than José was letting us have at the moment. I was the foreman. It was up to me to do something about the situation. But what?

I couldn't help thinking about Jessica. She always managed to find time for fun. How did she do it?

Suddenly I knew the answer. Jessica didn't just find time for fun—she *made* time. And that gave me a great idea.

I pulled Veronica aside and told her I had a plan. Her eyes lit up when I told her what it was, and she promised to help.

"What an awesome idea, Elizabeth," she said. "You're brilliant!"

I was feeling pretty brilliant too. And I was sure Jessica would be totally proud of me if she were here.

SATURDAY, 12:30 A.M.

Well, Diary, my plan is in action. Veronica, Kate, and I stayed in all evening and were awake half the night making our flyers, but it will all be worth it Monday night!

The flyers look really cool. They say Rain Forest Rave: Be There or Be Square! in English and Spanish. Then they have the time and place to meet. We're having the rave at a larger clearing just past the one with the little stream. Veronica suggested the place; she said it would be perfect. It's right off the main path, and she says that everyone knows where it is.

It was thinking about Jessica that inspired the idea for the rave. She loves to dance more than anything, and then of course there were those CDs she gave me. . . . It was sort of a natural, really. I figured, what could be more fun than a big, cool dance in the rain forest? OK, I know it's kind of bringing American culture here, which we weren't supposed to do. But after seeing how much Veronica loves American music, I figured the local kids would be into it. (And I'll admit it—the thought of possibly slow dancing with J.P. in a moonlit clearing made the idea seem even better!)

I was a little doubtful when Veronica said she wanted to invite José. He seemed kind of serious, and I was afraid he might give away our secret to the adults. But I just couldn't say no when she has such a huge crush on him. He didn't say much after we gave him the flyer, just sort of read it and nodded. I'm keeping my fingers crossed, and so is Veronica (for a different reason!).

MONDAY, *11:59* P.M.

Veronica, Jorge, Kate, and I slipped out of the house right after dinner and raced to the clearing. A few other helpers were already waiting for us there, including J.P. and Andy. We got things set up with the portable CD boom box we borrowed from the office shack and some tall torches Veronica found somewhere. I was a little nervous about the fire, but then Jorge pointed out that the vegetation is so wet right now that it's not a big danger. Plus we stuck them in the ground well away from any trees.

I was glad they talked me into it because the torches looked amazing. The firelight really made the clearing look cool. Plus it would have been hard to dance in the dark.

Finally everything was perfect. A folding table at the edge of the clearing groaned under the weight of sodas and snacks. The boom box sat on a smaller table with a stack of CDs beside it. The torches flickered and danced around the edges of the "dance floor," which was really just a wide, flat, grassy area of the clearing.

"It looks fantastic," J.P. declared. He let out a whoop. "Let's party!"

I laughed excitedly. His spirit was catching. "Hey, Veronica, why don't you do the honors?" I pointed at the boom box.

Veronica grinned. "Definitely." She stepped over to the table and popped in a disc. Within seconds loud music replaced the sounds of the rain forest. The pounding beat seemed to bounce off the trees and echo back from the canopy.

"Yeeee-ha!" J.P. crowed. He started dancing all by himself, and that was all it took. Soon the rest of us were dancing too.

I hardly noticed when the other kids started to show up. As the circle of sky visible above the clearing grew darker and darker, until the twinkling stars shone almost as brightly as the glowing torches, the clearing magically became more and more crowded. By the time I sat down on a fallen log to catch my breath and look around, there must have been twenty or thirty people packed into the clearing.

J.P. sat down next to me, breathing hard from his enthusiastic dancing. "Whew!" he exclaimed. "This is great. Looks like your idea was a huge success!"

"Thanks. I'm glad everyone is having fun." I scanned the crowds of happy kids, both Americans and Ticos. Suddenly my jaw dropped. "Call me crazy—," I began.

"You're crazy," J.P. said promptly.

I rolled my eyes and continued. "—but isn't that Andy dancing with Kate over there?"

J.P. looked where I was pointing. He grinned. "What do you know."

I could hardly believe my eyes. There was a fast song playing, but Kate and Andy had their hands locked together and were swaying gently to a slow beat that only they seemed to hear. They were gazing into each other's eyes and smiling. Come to think of it, Andy hadn't been staring at me all the time lately, and now I knew why!

"I never would have guessed that they liked each other," I commented. "I mean, Kate is so pretty and bubbly and sort of lighthearted, and Andy is so serious and shy."

J.P. shrugged. "You know what they say," he said, scooting a little closer to me on the log. "Opposites attract."

I smiled up at him shyly, wondering if he was going to kiss me. But at that moment Veronica rushed over to where we were sitting. She looked cuter than ever in the light from the torches, which picked up highlights in her dark hair and made her deep brown eyes sparkle. "Elizabeth!" she cried excitedly. "Guess who just got here?"

I turned to look at the path leading back toward the village. José was standing there, looking awkward and serious compared to the giddy dancers just a few yards away.

I winked at Veronica. "It looks like he needs someone to talk to," I commented.

"Definitely," J.P. put in. "You can't let your guest be a wallflower, Veronica."

Veronica giggled. "I'm on my way." She dashed off in José's direction, and seconds later she had him by the arm and was dragging him toward the dance floor, chattering nonstop the whole time.

"Come on," J.P. said, hopping to his feet and stretching down one hand to help me up. "I love this song. Let's boogie!"

I laughed and let him pull me toward the dance floor. We found a spot near the edge of the crowd, under the branches of a large, low-growing palm tree. For the next three or four songs we danced nonstop.

Then a slow, romantic song came on. I suspected Veronica had something to do with it; it was a ballad from one of her CDs that I knew was one of her favorites.

J.P. grabbed both my hands and pulled me close so he could wrap his arms around me. I put my arms around his waist and rested my head on his shoulder. It was wonderful. But about halfway through the song, it got even better. He tugged gently on my hair. I looked up, wondering if something was wrong. But as soon as we were face-to-face, he kissed me! It took me by surprise, but in the best possible way. As I kissed him back I could hardly believe it was happening—the incredible kiss, a dreamy ballad blasting from the CD player, the flickering torches, the lush rain forest surrounding us. . . . I couldn't imagine anything more romantic if I tried.

J.P. and I were so busy kissing that I didn't notice Tanya come up to us.

I saw her arrive a little earlier. She came along with some of the other kids from Gemelo, but she seemed determined not to have fun. She kept making snide little comments about how wrong it was to import American culture. What a hypocrite!

Now she came up beside J.P. and me and cleared her throat really loudly. "Glad to see you two are having fun," she said sarcastically.

J.P. pulled away from me and gave her an annoyed look. "Oh, hi, Tanya," he said. "I'm surprised you recognize fun when you see it. You must have learned something on this trip after all."

I was wishing she would go away and leave us alone so J.P. and I could get back to what we were doing. But she seemed to have no intention of leaving anytime soon. She was standing with her arms folded and one foot tapping impatiently.

"What do you want, Tanya?" I asked, feeling pretty impatient myself.

"I want to talk to you, Elizabeth," she replied

evenly. "I have something important to say."

Somehow as soon as she said that I knew exactly what she wanted to talk about: She had figured out my little prank from the other night. I gulped. I should have known she would recognize the CDs we were playing and figure it out.

I realized that I couldn't let J.P. know the truth. Everyone thought Tanya had returned the gas cap on her own. If he found out I took it, he might guess that was the whole reason I snuck over there. Then he would go back to thinking all I care about is working hard and winning the contest. And he might stop liking me, which I definitely didn't want to happen.

I gave J.P. what I hoped was a flirtatious look. "Hey, J.P.," I said. "Uh—all that dancing made me really thirsty. Would you mind getting me a soda while I talk to Tanya for a second?"

He tried to argue, talking about the romantic moment and the great song and some other stuff. I don't really remember his exact words because the whole time I had the uncomfortable feeling that he was saying it all to make Tanya jealous.

Eventually he left, though, and Tanya and I were alone under the palm fronds.

Tanya was furious. She'd hidden it when J.P. was there, but now she really let it out. At first her words were so jumbled and angry that I had trouble following them. But I soon realized that she had guessed the truth.

"I know you put that snake in my tent," she spat out finally. "And I know you stole the gas cap and those CDs."

My heart was pounding nervously. For the first time I realized how bad it sounded when you said it straight out like that.

Then I remembered that the situation wasn't that simple. Tanya had stolen that gas cap herself; I was just returning it to where it belonged. And the CDs and magazines had been mine to begin with.

I reminded her of those things, managing to sound a lot calmer than I felt.

"I know all that," Tanya snapped, her eyes still flashing fire. "I'm not an idiot. I know I can't squeal even if I wanted to." Tanya glanced around to make sure no one was listening. Then she leaned a little closer. "I just want you to know that I know," she said in a low, nasty voice. "And I want you to know that I'm going to get back at you for what you've done. Somehow."

Before I could say another word, she stalked away and disappeared into the crowd. I bit my lip and stared after her, wondering what she had in mind. What could she do to me? She wouldn't dare risk getting in trouble and losing that Outstanding Volunteer award.

*She's probably just trying to scare me,* I told myself, hoping it was true. A second later J.P. reappeared and reported that the sodas were gone, and I had to pretend that everything was fine while we figured out what to do about getting more refreshments.

I managed to forget about Tanya's threat—mostly anyway—and have fun for the rest of the evening. We would probably still be out there dancing if Mr. Herrera and a few of the other adults from the village hadn't come to break it up. I guess we hadn't kept the secret as well as we'd thought. They were very cool about it, though—Mr. Herrera even asked Kate and me to dance with him for the last song. It was a fast one, and the three of us joined hands and skipped around in a circle. It was silly but fun. Halfway through, Veronica and Jorge came running over and pushed their way into the circle, and then J.P. and Andy and a few other kids from our village joined us too. Before long half the people in the clearing were holding hands and dancing around together. It was a perfect way to end the night.

Well, almost end it, that is.

After the last dance the adults shooed most of the kids home. Soon only Veronica, Jorge, Andy, Kate, J.P., and I were left. With the help of Mr. Herrera and the other adults, we set about cleaning up the clearing. Veronica had already spirited the CDs into a bag she had brought with her and was now packing away the leftover food. Andy and Kate were working together to extinguish and gather the torches. Jorge and his father were folding up the refreshments table.

I looked around for something to do. Noticing the

boom box, I walked over and grabbed it. "I'm going to return this to the office shack," I said. "I can take the table back there too, if someone will help me."

I had someone in particular in mind, and luckily he's pretty quick to take a hint. "I've got it," J.P. said. He grabbed the table and folded down the legs. "Let's go."

"I think everything's under control here," Mr. Herrera called to us as we left the clearing. "So we'll just meet you two back at the village."

"Right," Veronica called out in a singsong voice. "Don't be long, you two!"

I blushed, but I didn't really mind her teasing. J.P. grinned at me and winked.

The two of us didn't talk much as we headed through the forest toward the village. But it still felt really romantic as we strolled along after such an incredible evening.

When we got to the office shack, I unlocked the door and we both went inside. J.P. set the CD player on the desk, then turned to face me.

I felt my heart start to beat faster as he looked at me, then took a step closer. I thought he was going to kiss me, but instead he spoke. "You're really something special, Elizabeth," he said softly.

"You are too," I replied.

"I can't believe I didn't even know you two weeks ago." J.P. shook his head.

"J.P.," I said hesitantly. "There's something I want to ask you. It's about Tanya."

"Tanya?" he repeated. "What about her?"

I felt like kicking myself for bringing it up, but it was too late. Besides, if Tanya was going to hold a grudge against me, I had to know why. And it would have been obvious that there was some history between her and J.P. even if Kate hadn't told me.

"Kate told me that the two of you used to go out. But it seems like there's still some angry feelings between the two of you. Do you think she's mad at me because of you?"

J.P. nodded thoughtfully. "It's possible," he admitted. He didn't look angry or annoyed that I had brought up Tanya's name. Just sort of sad. "When I first got to know her, I thought Tanya was really cool," he said. "But she started to change. She was always talking about school and grades and boring stuff like that. She never wanted to just kick back and have fun anymore."

"Oh." I felt a little weird, hearing that. I couldn't help remembering how J.P. had acted when he thought I was just a serious, boring goody-goody.

"That wasn't really why we broke up, though," he went on. Now he did look kind of angry. "It was something she did. Last year in art class I built a scale model of a city—I worked on it for two months. It was no bigger than a chessboard. My art teacher talked me into entering it in our school's fine arts fair."

I remembered that Kate had mentioned something

about J.P.'s award-winning project. "You won, didn't you?"

"Yes—no thanks to Tanya." J.P. shook his head grimly. "The night before the contest she came to my house to hang out. We had been sitting on the porch, and Tanya excused herself to go to the bathroom. I decided that I wanted to show the city to her—she had seen me working on it but hadn't seen it finished yet. When I went to get the city, which was locked away in my dad's study so nobody would touch it—I got there just in time to see her holding my cat above it." He paused and glanced at me. "She was going to drop the cat on the city. The project would have been ruined, and I never would have known she'd done it. Boots would have taken all the blame."

I gasped. I had already guessed that Tanya was competitive. But now I realized it went beyond that—she was downright ruthless. "Why would she do that?" I cried.

"Isn't it obvious? She wanted to win that fair herself." He shrugged. "But never mind Tanya." He moved closer and took my hands in his own. "I don't want to think about her. Not when I'm standing here with you."

He kissed me softly. But just then we heard voices coming and realized we'd better go before we got caught.

It was just as well. My mind was swirling with what he'd told me. If Tanya would do something so sneaky to her own boyfriend, what would she do to me?

But that wasn't all I was worried about. I kept thinking about J.P. and me. Why did he like me anyway? Was I really the fun-loving girl he thought I was—the kind of girl who organizes a rave in the rain forest? Or was I the kind of person he thought I was after Marion's little speech about me—a dull overachiever who only cares about grades and being the best? I thought the second description was closer to the truth—at least it had been until recently.

But maybe I'm changing now. Maybe this trip is helping me to become a different kind of person. And maybe that's a good thing. I'm starting to think I was so serious before that I never really let myself open up to a guy, not even Todd Wilkins. Now that I've met J.P., I finally know what I was missing.

After all, what good are brains and good grades and achievements without heart and soul and *fun*?

# *Eight*

◇

It was kind of anticlimactic slogging along on our construction job after the excitement of the Rain Forest Rave. Robert and Marion stopped by late in the morning. They'd heard about the rave from some kids in Gemelo. I wouldn't be surprised if Tanya had something to do with that. Robert gave us a long, disapproving lecture. He said we're supposed to be here working, not partying.

At the end he turned to look at me. For a second I was afraid he was going to punish me for being the one who planned the rave. But I guess he didn't know it was me. He just told me I need to keep a closer eye on things so this doesn't happen again. That struck me as incredibly funny, and I had a hard time holding back my giggles until after he and Marion drove off. I wasn't the only one. As soon as the two adults were gone all the kids started laughing.

Then we got back to work. Everyone was kind of sleepy after our late night, but we did our best. A little while after Robert and Marion left, José turned up to see how we were doing. He told us the support beams and exterior walls should all be up by the day after tomorrow. Then he said he'd be back in a couple of days to check on us. Veronica had just showed up to help (she slept in this morning—lucky her!) and looked really disappointed that he was leaving.

Nothing much happened for the next couple of hours. We stopped for lunch, then got back to work on the support beams as José had instructed.

I realized I needed to bring out a bunch of tools from the office shack, so I asked J.P. to help me get them. We went inside and started grabbing the stuff we needed.

That was when I saw them. Along with the boards and sheets of metal and other junk piled on one side of the office shack, there was a huge pile of old tires—the kind that float—inner tubes. Suddenly a little lightbulb went on in my mind.

"Hey, J.P.," I said casually. "I just had a truly fabulous idea."

He turned, saw me staring at the inner tubes, and immediately guessed what I had in mind.

"You're not thinking about blowing off work this afternoon to go tubing, are you?" he said.

"Why not?" I was a little surprised that he sounded so hesitant. "We're all so tired from the rave that we probably won't get much done anyway. And this way we'll be happy and well rested so we can get back to work fresh and eager tomorrow."

The reasons just popped out, as if someone else had thought of them for me. It all seemed to make such perfect sense that I was amazed J.P. couldn't see it too.

He still looked a little bit worried. "Yeah, but José said . . ."

I did my best to copy that little pout Jessica always uses when a guy isn't doing what she wants him to do. "Hey, if you want to hang out with José, be my guest," I teased. "But if you want to hang out with me . . ."

"OK, OK," he said with a laugh. "You're the boss, right?"

He still didn't seem totally enthusiastic. But that wore off pretty quickly once we gathered the rest of the gang and headed for the river. Veronica and Jorge showed us a fantastic stretch of river for tubing. We spent the entire afternoon floating along, having splash fights, dunking each other, and generally having a great time.

Between all that exercise and our lack of sleep, we were all pretty worn out by dinnertime. I almost fell asleep in my soup. But it was worth it. The adults didn't suspect a thing—they think we spent the day at the building site.

And we still have all day tomorrow to make up the work we missed. It shouldn't be a problem—it will be sort of like the way Jessica always leaves all her weekend homework until nine o'clock Sunday night. She has to rush to get it done, but she always manages to pull it off somehow. All we have to do is work a little longer tomorrow to make up for today.

*WEDNESDAY, 9:10 P.M.*

I found out the most exciting thing this morning! Today was market day in San Sebastián. It happens once a month—people from Valle Dulce, Gemelo, and about half a dozen other nearby villages gather in San Sebastián's main square for a full day of eating, shopping, and socializing.

"It is awesome, *macha*," Veronica told me over breakfast. "Everyone goes and has a blast. There are tons of food booths, crafts, musicians, boat rides, performing monkeys and parrots, and all sorts of other cool stuff to do and see."

By the time she finished describing it, I had made up my mind. "We have to find a way to go!" I told Veronica and Jorge when their parents were out of earshot. "How can we get there? San Sebastián must be at least ten miles away—we'd need a ride."

Veronica grinned and exchanged a glance with Jorge. "I'll see what I can do."

As soon as I got to the construction site I told everyone about the market. "Veronica is going to try to find us a ride," I added. "Who's in?"

Most of the kids seemed pretty psyched about the whole idea. Tiffany, Kate, and Anne immediately started discussing all the shopping they wanted to do. Ty started asking questions about the boat rides I'd mentioned. Andy wondered aloud if he would be able to find a book on local birds and plants.

I glanced at J.P., expecting him to be as excited as everyone else. But he was frowning. "We're supposed to have the support beams and walls up by the end of the day," he said.

I had been expecting someone to bring that up. But I was surprised that it was J.P. Luckily I had an answer ready for him. "No problemo," I said with a grin. "We've got Coco on our side!"

You see, that morning I had remembered the Web page I'd printed out. It had all sorts of useful tips for saving time and money.

I passed it around the group, explaining exactly what we needed to do. "If we follow the tips and work as fast as we can," I finished, "I figure we can have the walls and beams up in less than two hours."

"Then what are we waiting for?" Ty called out. "Let's go!"

We got to work. A few of the others were a little worried at first because we weren't following José's instructions. But they relaxed once they saw how well Coco's methods were working. And how *quickly* they were working.

While the rest of us were busy at the site, Veronica managed to track down a high-school-age friend who agreed to drive us all into San Sebastián. By the time a battered, rust-blotched green van pulled up to the construction site, we were putting the finishing touches on the walls.

"All right!" J.P. shouted as he hammered in one last nail. "That should do it. Is everyone ready for fun?"

While the others cheered and dropped their tools, I grinned. "Last one in the van is a rotten guava!"

When we got to San Sebastián, there were mobs of people in the town square, talking, laughing, eating, buying things. Veronica and Jorge spotted some friends from school and rushed over to say hello. Kate and Andy wandered toward a nearby food stall. The others scattered every which way.

"Where do you want to start?" J.P. asked, grabbing my hand.

I squeezed back. "I want to see it all!" I declared.

He grinned. "Let's go!"

We plunged into the crowd, trying to take in everything at once. First we stopped for a quick snack at a stand that sold something called *cajeta de coco.* It tasted sort of like fudge, and it had coconut in it and I don't know what else. Then we moved on to a section of the square devoted to local crafts and other gift items. I found lots of great souvenirs for people back home. I bought a woven shirt for Jess (purple, her favorite color), some local crafts for Mom and Dad, a hat for Steven, cute little tree frog pins for Maria and a few other friends, and a hand-carved flute for myself. J.P. liked Steven's hat so much that he got one just like it for himself. At one booth we saw a cool movie poster that we were sure Veronica would like, so we both chipped in to get it for her. By that time we were carrying so much stuff, we couldn't hold hands anymore. But we were having a fantastic time.

After a while we went looking for Veronica. It wasn't easy to track her down in the crowd, but somehow we found her. She was thrilled by the movie poster.

"It is so awesome!" she exclaimed. "I must figure out a really cool place to hang it up."

J.P. wanted to go watch some boat races that were just starting, so I decided to walk around with Veronica for a while. We tossed the stuff we'd bought into her friend's van, which was parked on a narrow side street nearby, then headed back toward the square.

That was when we had our first bit of bad luck all day. Veronica and I were turning the corner to reenter the square when we saw José walking toward us, a frown on his face. It was too late to run. He'd spotted us.

"What are you two doing here?" he demanded.

I gulped. I knew José would never approve of using Coco's shortcuts, even if it made perfect sense. We had to come up with an excuse he would believe.

I glanced at Veronica, but she was no help. She was gazing at José with a goofy, adoring smile on her face. I was on my own.

"No problemo, José," I said, thinking quickly. "Um, the work is progressing steadily back at the village."

Veronica looked at me, seeming surprised. Before she could say anything to give us away, I went on.

"So," I said to José. "What are you doing here?"

I was hoping to distract José from his own question by changing the subject. Jessica does that all the time. Mom and Dad are usually too smart to fall for it, but it always works on Steven.

"I came to bargain for some copper wire," José replied. "But you have not answered my question. Why are you two here?"

"It's OK, José," I said smoothly. "The work is going so well that we figured we had time to come over and pick up some . . . uh . . . gravel. We were going to surprise Marion and Robert by building a path from the road to the front door."

"Oh." José thought about that for a second while

I held my breath. "Then the beams and walls will be finished by the end of the day?"

I let out the breath I was holding. "Oh, yes. I can practically guarantee it," I assured him. "The rest of the crew is back at the village hard at work."

I heard Veronica let out a little gasp, and out of the corner of my eye I saw what she had just seen. Andy and Kate were strolling past just a few yards away at the edge of the market square, hand in hand. They were so wrapped up in each other that they didn't even notice us—or José.

I froze. José was facing away from them right now, but he could turn his head at any moment. As soon as he saw Kate and Andy he would realize I'd been lying.

Veronica saved the day. She grabbed José by the hand.

"Listen, I never got a chance to tell you what a radical time I had with you at the rave," she said, fluttering her dark eyelashes at him. "Thanks a million. It was totally awesome and . . . *romantic*."

It was obvious that José had no idea what to say. He stared at Veronica blankly for a second, his face slowly turning pink. "I too enjoyed—er, that is— you are quite—um . . ." He paused, clearly completely tongue-tied. "I must get my wire," he finished at last, his face bright red by now.

I quickly checked the spot where Kate and Andy had been, but they were gone. Whew! It had worked!

"We will come along and keep you company," Veronica told José, following as he hurried toward the square. "Right, Elizabeth?"

I guessed what she was thinking. We might need to distract him again if we ran into anyone else from the crew. I was tempted to leave the job to Veronica alone. She obviously knew exactly how to distract José. Still, I was afraid she might get distracted herself and forget to keep a lookout for the others. So I tagged along, feeling like a third wheel but not really minding too much.

It wasn't easy, but we did it. For a while it seemed that every time we turned around, someone else from the crew popped into sight. First it was J.P., who was still watching the boat races. He spotted us at the same time I spotted him. I nudged Veronica. She took José by the arm, which distracted him more than long enough for J.P. to back away into the crowd, out of sight.

We encountered Kate and Andy again too. They were sitting on a bench at the edge of the square, eating what looked like tortillas. Andy's eyes widened when he saw us, and I was afraid he was going to choke on his tortilla. But Kate grabbed his arm and dragged him out of sight behind a craft stand while Veronica stood on tiptoes to whisper something into a blushing and completely distracted José's ear.

When I noticed Jorge heading in our direction, I wasn't sure what to do since he wasn't officially a part of the crew. Still, I decided it would be better if José had no reason to be suspicious at all. So I poked Veronica on the shoulder, and she gave José a big, impulsive hug as Jorge quickly changed directions and melted into the crowd.

I can't remember how many times we had to repeat our little game. But finally I guess José got so overwhelmed by Veronica's attention that he had to leave. He quickly bought his copper wire and mumbled something about getting back to work. I'm not sure if he was talking about himself or us. We walked him back to his car. And just before he got in, he blushed deep red, then leaned over and gave Veronica a lightning-fast kiss on the forehead before leaping into the front seat and driving off at top speed.

Maybe with most guys that wouldn't seem like much, but coming from José it was practically a wedding proposal. Veronica was so happy, she just drifted around the market for the rest of the day in her own dream world. Every time J.P. and I saw her, she blew us kisses and grinned her head off.

There's no doubt about it—romance is in the air!

# Nine

◇

Tanya never gives up.

Lucky me, I hadn't seen her since the rave. But tonight she came over to Valle Dulce after dinner. I had just left the house to look for J.P. when I ran into her.

She had just been to the construction site, and she clearly wasn't pleased with what she saw there. She was totally nasty to me and also to Kate and Andy, who happened to be standing nearby, examining the large orchid plant growing on the side of the Herreras' house.

"You guys think you're so great," Tanya spat out, crossing her arms. "But I heard you've been goofing off every day." She glared at me. "I can't figure out how you can give your crew so much time off and still get your work done. There's something going on, and I plan to find out what it is."

"Maybe Elizabeth's just a better leader than you are," Andy said loyally.

"That's right," Kate added. "Maybe you should take lessons from her, Tanya."

Tanya tossed her head and stalked away without answering, heading back toward Gemelo. A minute or two later J.P. came by, and I forgot all about Tanya.

But later, when I thought about her visit again, I felt pretty annoyed. It was obvious that she only came over to see how our work compares to hers. Maybe she *should* take some lessons from me and my crew—lessons on how to lighten up and have some fun. After all, we're proving that we can finish everything we need to do and still take time to enjoy ourselves. It's too bad she can't learn the same thing.

*Sunday, 9:20 P.M.*

Coco is the greatest!

Sorry I haven't had much time to write in the past couple of days, Diary. I've been too busy. After the success of market day I realized just how useful Coco's Cost-Cutting Construction Concepts could be. On Friday, Coco's tips saved us so much time that we finished all our tasks by lunchtime, so we spent the whole afternoon in the rain forest. I'm not sure what the others did, but J.P. and I hung out in "our" clearing for most of the day. Yesterday afternoon we finished in time to go hear a local band Veronica knew about at a village a couple of miles away.

And the best part is, our building is going great! Robert and Marion stopped by today and seemed impressed. They said that everything looked perfect.

Who knew being superefficient would be so easy? Not to mention so much fun!

*WEDNESDAY, 9:58 P.M.*

Sorry, Diary—I know I should be writing every day, but I just can't seem to keep up. But I have really good excuses. The other day, after Marion and Robert left, we all knocked off work early for a lizard-catching contest. It was Veronica's idea. J.P. and I worked as a team, but we didn't do very well. We only caught three lizards. The "prize"—a crown Veronica made out of leaves and vines—went to Andy, who caught seven. Kate gave him a big kiss to congratulate him, which I guess was an even better prize than the crown, judging by the look on his face.

We've done a bunch of other fun stuff in the past few days too. One afternoon we found a coconut grove and Jorge tried to teach us how to climb the tall, skinny trunks. J.P. got about eight feet up and then slid down. He scraped his elbow pretty badly, but as soon as I kissed it he claimed it felt totally better. We also snuck out the CD player again and had a sing-along and dance contest. Yesterday Veronica took us to the beach to look for nesting turtles.

Whoever first said that all work and no play makes you dull must have been a genius. We're all having tons of fun, and the work is going great. José stopped by yesterday, and he seemed really pleased with our progress. He even singled out Veronica, praising her for pitching in to help with the work. He said he used to think she was "flighty" but that I was obviously a good influence on her. Believe me, Veronica and I had a good laugh over that one after he left! If anyone has been influenced lately, it's me. Veronica and J.P. have helped show me that having fun is just as important as being serious and responsible. I just hope I remember that in a few weeks when I start eighth grade!

*FRIDAY, 10:10 P.M.*

It's hard to believe my Costa Rican adventure is almost over. We're flying home in just over a week, next Saturday to be exact. Part of me feels like I just got here, while the other part feels like I've been here forever. I have to admit, I am really starting to miss home—the people, the food, even the TV. I wonder how Jessica is doing? I can't believe I haven't spoken to her in almost four weeks!

But I'll see her and everybody else before too much longer. What I'm thinking about more right now is how much I'll miss these incredible times in the rain forest with J.P. and the rest of my new friends.

Yesterday afternoon J.P. and I stole away to celebrate the two-week anniversary of the day we got together—that day that everything changed between us. It was really romantic. J.P. surprised me with a bunch of tropical flowers he'd gathered from the rain forest. Then we relived our first kiss. It was so wonderful—something I'm sure I'll remember for the rest of my life. Just like I'll remember everything else about this wonderful trip.

The community center is almost finished, mostly thanks to Coco's Construction Concepts. When José stopped by yesterday, he could hardly believe how much we had done. He promised to bring Marion and Robert back with him tomorrow to see it. Meanwhile Jorge went over to the other village this morning and found out that Tanya's house isn't anywhere near finished.

Could life possibly get any better than this?

# Ten

I should have known it was all too good to last.

Here's what happened. We got started extra early at the construction site this morning since we knew that Robert, Marion, and José would be stopping by. And our hard work paid off. By the time they pulled up at the site, the new community center was pretty much finished.

It still needed some paint and a few other finishing touches, of course. But the building part was done, and that was the important thing—the part we were brought to do. Robert and Marion were incredibly impressed.

"You kids have been one of the best work crews we've ever seen," Robert declared, stepping back and looking over the building as we all watched. "I can't believe you did so much so fast."

"Me either," Marion agreed. "You guys have done a fantastic job." Her eyes twinkled as she glanced at us. "That's why we've already decided to have a big party to celebrate the completion of the community center."

I gasped in surprise along with the rest of my crew.

"A party?" J.P. cried. "Cool!"

Marion grinned. "Robert and José and I already told the kids from Gemelo that they should quit work early today and come over. Your host families have offered to make some refreshments." She paused to wait for the excited whoops and shouts to die down before continuing. "So by the time you all finish cleaning up the site and putting the tools away, it will be time to celebrate!"

I noticed that even Robert didn't look as serious as usual. In fact, he looked thrilled. "I'm so proud of you all," he said. He paused and traded a glance with Marion. "By the way, we've been considering having our award presentation this afternoon. I think it's pretty obvious who the outstanding volunteer should be."

Veronica elbowed me in the ribs. I blushed and smiled as Robert winked at me.

"OK, everyone," I said in my best foreman's voice. "Let's get those tools put away!" We all scattered to do our part as José and the adults hurried down the path toward the village.

I was helping Kate gather up a pile of leftover two-by-fours when J.P. found me. "Well, well," he said. "I wonder who Robert could have meant just now? Do you two have any idea?"

"I don't know," I joked. "But if you ask me, we should give the award to Coco."

Kate giggled. "Truc. We *could* have done it without those concepts . . ."

". . . but we couldn't have had this much fun while we did it," I finished, raising my hand for a high five.

By late afternoon the party was in full swing. All the American kids and a lot of Ticos from both Valle Dulce and Gemelo came, bringing food and drinks and even some more CDs. Everyone gathered in the clearing in front of the new community center and started eating, dancing, and having a great time. I stuffed myself with delicious Costa Rican food, then headed for the area near the boom box to work it off.

I started dancing with J.P., but before long the other boys from my crew started cutting in. I ended up dancing with all of them at least twice. I even danced with Duane, who had come over with the other kids from Gemelo. He only stepped on my foot once, and he hardly talked about *Star Trek* at all.

I was having a great time. The only dark spot was Tanya. Anytime I went within ten yards of her, she glared at me like she thought she could turn me to stone or something. I wasn't surprised, but it was still kind of unnerving. I wasn't exactly comfortable with the thought that she obviously hated me so much. *Who cares?* I told myself at one point. *Let her stare all she wants. She's just jealous because she knows she'll never win that award now.*

The sun was beginning to set when Robert hopped onto the front steps of the new community center and clapped. "May I have your attention, please?" he said. Then he repeated his words in Spanish.

Someone turned off the CD player, and we all started gathering around him. I felt my heart start to pound nervously as I guessed what was coming. J.P. must have guessed too—he squeezed my hand and winked at me.

When everyone was listening, Robert went on, still repeating his words in both English and Spanish. "As you can see, your beautiful new community center is finished—and well ahead of schedule." He smiled at all of us from the work crew before continuing. "Our student volunteers have done a wonderful job, and we congratulate them. And now, on behalf of the Rain Forest Friends organization, Marion and I would like to present this award to the volunteer who has done the most to make this day possible." He held up a shiny wooden plaque. "I am very pleased to present this honor to our Valle Dulce team foreman—Miss Elizabeth Wakefield!"

My crew erupted into loud whoops and cheers.

All the Ticos and most of the volunteers from Gemelo joined in.

As I walked toward Robert to accept my award I glanced around for Tanya, wondering how she was taking this. But she was nowhere in sight, and I soon forgot about her as Robert handed me the polished wooden plaque. It had the Rain Forest Friends logo carved onto it along with the name of the village and the date and the words *Outstanding Volunteer.*

"Thank you—*muchas gracias*," I said as I accepted it. "This is a great honor. But I want everyone to know that I never could have done it without my wonderful crew—J.P., Kate, Andy, Ty, Tiffany, Loren, Will, Sumi, Ricky, Anne, and Bridget, and of course our honorary crew members Veronica and Jorge Herrera. You're the best, guys! Let's give them a big hand."

The crowd cheered loudly as my crew grinned and waved. Since everyone still seemed to be expecting a speech, I said a few more words, thanking Marion, Robert, and José and wishing the villagers many years of pleasure from their new community center. Then I stepped down to the sounds of more cheering, feeling a little embarrassed at all the attention but happy at the same time.

The music started up again, and J.P. and I got right back to dancing.

That's when I noticed Tanya. I happened to be

facing the office shack when she suddenly emerged from behind it. *What was she doing back there?* I wondered idly. I smiled as I answered my own question. *Probably hiding out so she didn't have to watch me accept that award.*

Feeling a tiny bit guilty about my mean thought, I glanced at her again. This time I noticed that she wasn't scowling like she had been all afternoon. In fact, she had a strange sort of half smile on her face.

*What's that all about?* I wondered. For some reason her expression suddenly made me kind of nervous. She looked like a cat who had just swallowed the world's most delicious canary.

I craned my neck to get a better look, but just then Ricky and Sumi danced by, blocking my view. I took a step to the side, trying to see where Tanya was going.

"What are you doing?" J.P. asked, moving aside to match my steps.

I jumped. I had almost forgotten where I was. "Oh, nothing," I lied. For some reason I didn't want to tell him the truth.

At that moment Ty danced past and punched J.P. on the arm, and J.P. turned to chat with him. That gave me the chance to look for Tanya again. I spotted her over by the boom box, whispering something to José.

I watched as the two of them headed toward the office shack, with Tanya leading the way. José was frowning, and Tanya looked happier than ever. But just then Marion shouted for everyone's attention. I saw that Veronica was standing beside her, grinning from ear to ear.

"Sorry to interrupt," Marion said cheerfully once someone had turned off the music once again. "But I thought it would be fun to do something to christen your new community center. And Veronica Herrera has just generously volunteered to donate a brand-new poster, which will be hung to decorate the main room." She held up the movie poster that J.P. and I had bought Veronica at the market.

*How sweet of her!* I thought. When Veronica glanced over at me, I gave her a thumbs-up.

"What a cool idea," J.P. whispered to me, his warm breath tickling my ear a little. "It's perfect— Veronica will probably spend a ton of time at the community center anyway, so she'll still get to enjoy the poster."

"And what could be more appropriate," Marion went on, "than for our award-winning team foreman to have the honor of hanging the poster. Elizabeth? How about it?"

"Sure," I called out with a smile. "But only if Veronica will help me!"

Someone handed me a small hammer and the poster, and someone else gave Veronica a couple of tacks. Then the two of us went into our new building. There wasn't enough room inside for everyone, so the rest of the party goers crowded around outside the wide windows to watch.

I held the poster against one wall. "How does this look?"

"Majorly awesome!" Veronica exclaimed. She stepped forward and poked one tack through the corner of the poster into the wall. I raised the hammer.

"Here goes!" I cried gleefully. I swung the hammer and hit the tack square on the head—once, twice, three times. "OK," I said. "Next tack, please, Veron—"

That was all I had time for. Because just then, with a creaking, cracking, groaning, splintering sound, the wall with the poster on it tipped forward—and started to fall right toward us!

Veronica and I both screamed and jumped back, trying our best to cover our heads. I don't think I've ever been so scared in my life. It seemed as though the whole building was collapsing right on top of us! Everyone watching must have been pretty worried too because I could hear gasps and shrieks and cries from all around.

A second later, with a loud *crash*, the top part of the wall smashed to the ground—right in front of the door. Veronica and I were trapped.

Luckily no more of the building seemed ready to collapse. So we just stood there, in the middle of a community center that suddenly had only three and a half walls instead of four, with the entire population of two villages and all the student volunteers looking in at us.

Their faces were still worried at first. But we must have looked pretty silly standing there with hammer in hand and broken pieces of wall at our feet. Because after a few seconds of stunned silence there was a nervous titter from somewhere in the crowd. That was all it took. Everyone burst out laughing.

My face was so red, it felt like it was going to burn off. Veronica looked really embarrassed too. But I knew she couldn't possibly be feeling the same amount of humiliation and shame I was feeling. She wasn't the team foreman. She hadn't been responsible. She wasn't the—gasp!—"outstanding volunteer" who had led the way in building this defective community center.

"What in the world is going on here?" I heard Marion cry from somewhere outside. "What happened?"

"Maybe Elizabeth huffed and puffed and blew the house down!" shouted some joker whose voice I didn't recognize.

"This is no laughing matter," Robert's stern voice broke in through the laughter. A moment later I saw his face poking in through the window. "Girls, are you hurt?"

Veronica and I shook our heads. Then we went to the window, and Robert helped us climb through it.

Once I was outside, I noticed that not everyone was laughing. The other members of my crew looked just as embarrassed as Veronica and I did. Andy's face was flaming, and Kate's big blue eyes were watery. J.P. was frowning, and most of the others looked either ashamed or confused.

I also noticed something else. Tanya had returned and was pushing her way to the front of the crowd. José was behind her, looking grim.

Andy saw Tanya too. He spun around and pointed at her. "She did it!" he shouted. "Tanya sabotaged our building. She'll do anything to win!"

There were murmurs of surprise from the crowd. Even Tanya looked startled at Andy's words.

Robert frowned. "That's a serious accusation, Andy," he said severely. "Do you have any proof of what you're saying?"

Kate was tugging on Andy's arm, obviously trying to calm him down. But he wasn't paying any attention to her.

"Elizabeth didn't want me to tell anyone," he said. "But Tanya was the one who stole that gas cap the very first week. She wanted to make the truck late so her team would get a head start."

Tanya gasped. "You . . . you . . . ," she sputtered angrily, glaring at me.

But Andy wasn't finished. "She wants to win, no matter what. But there's no way I'm going to let her make Elizabeth look bad like this!" He waved his hand at the half-collapsed building. "Not after she worked so hard and was such a great foreman!"

My cheeks were still flaming, though now it was as much from shame as from embarrassment. I knew the truth, even if poor Andy was too clueless to see it. Tanya hadn't had anything to do with the wall collapsing. It was my fault—because I wasn't a great foreman at all. I wasn't even an adequate foreman. I was a horrible one. I had cared more about having fun and sneaking off to hang with J.P. than I had about doing a good job. Why hadn't I seen it sooner?

I glanced over at J.P. to see what he was thinking. He was staring back at me, his eyes narrowed and his face thoughtful.

I gulped, knowing that he was finally figuring out what had happened. All this time he'd thought I put that snake in Tanya's tent as a funny way of getting revenge. That's what I had let him think. But Andy's words had reminded him about that stupid gas cap. You wouldn't have to be as smart as J.P. to put two and two together and realize that I took back the gas cap to get the project moving.

I wanted a chance to talk to him, to explain. But just then José spoke up. His face was like a stone. "I have something to show you," he told Robert and Marion. "Come with me."

Robert and Marion followed him, and the rest of us drifted along behind them. Veronica fell into step beside me, looking nervous. "What happened?" she whispered.

I didn't know what to tell her. I just shook my head and shrugged helplessly, hating the nervous look on her normally happy face. *Could this day possibly get any worse?* I wondered.

Naturally the answer to that question was yes.

José brought Robert and Marion to the supply pile at the back of the office shack. As soon as the adults saw it their faces darkened.

The day had definitely just gotten a *lot* worse. There was way too much stuff left over—too many extra nails, struts, supports, and everything else. Now the adults knew that we'd cut corners. *Why didn't we hide the extra supplies?* I thought desperately. But even as I thought it, I knew that wouldn't have done any good. They would have figured it out soon enough anyway.

Why did I ever believe that someone named Coco would know anything about construction?

There was a tense moment of silence. Then Robert, Marion, and José all started yelling at once, mostly at me. What could I have been thinking? Why hadn't I followed their instructions? How could I be so irresponsible? Etc., etc., etc.

"I know what she was thinking," J.P. broke in after a moment, pushing his way to the front of the crowd. "Actually, I just figured it out." He stared at me, his face white and his expression cold. "Elizabeth wanted to get our building up first. That's all she cared about all this time."

His angry words stung so much that I felt tears

spring to my eyes. "No, that's not true," I protested weakly.

"This was all about beating Tanya." J.P. had turned away from me by now, as if he couldn't stand to look at me anymore. He spoke to the adults. "About winning. I can't believe she's so competitive and selfish she would actually build an unsafe community center. But I guess it's true. We were idiots to trust her—all of us."

With that he shook his head in disgust and hurried away without another glance in my direction. I wanted to run after him, but I didn't dare. I had to handle the construction situation first. Still, it was breaking my heart to know that J.P. thought I'd betrayed him—just like Tanya had.

Robert and Marion took over then, ordering the rest of the kids to keep quiet. "We'll need some time to figure out what to do," Marion announced.

"I don't need any time," Robert declared angrily, turning to glare at me. "I know exactly what we should do."

I felt my whole body start to shake. *This is it,* I thought. *He's going to send me home. And he's going to do it in front of the whole village.*

I knew it was only what I deserved. But that didn't make it any easier to face.

Marion grabbed Robert by the arm. "Wait," she said. "Let's not be hasty. We should talk about this." She glanced at me. "Elizabeth, you'd better return to the Herreras' house now."

Robert didn't look particularly happy about that, but he didn't argue. And I didn't give Marion a chance to change her mind. I turned and raced for home, grateful to escape all those accusing, disappointed, and confused faces.

Halfway there I heard footsteps running after me. *J.P.?* I wondered, my heart jumping nervously. Maybe he had realized he had been unfair. Maybe he was following me to apologize and offer his support.

But when I turned, I discovered that it was Veronica who had followed me. "Elizabeth!" she gasped. "Wait! I want to come with you."

I was so happy to see her that I forgot all about J.P. I held out my arms, and she grabbed me in a big hug. She didn't say another word, but she didn't have to. I could tell that I had at least one friend left in this village.

We continued to her house and huddled in the guest room, wondering what would happen next.

"They can't send you home," Veronica kept repeating. "They just can't."

"Of course they can," I told her sadly. "Robert was practically frothing at the mouth to do it. And I don't blame him one bit. I really messed up."

"But you did your best," Veronica argued loyally.

I just shook my head, feeling too sick at heart to answer. She was being a good friend, but I knew the truth. I hadn't done my best. Not even close. I had let having a good time get in the way of doing a good job, and now everyone knew it. Why hadn't I recognized that until it was too late?

A little while later there was a knock on the door and Jorge stuck his head in. "There you are," he said.

Veronica jumped up and ran to her brother. "What's happening?" she demanded anxiously.

Jorge shook his head. "It is not good news." He sat down on the bed next to me and gave me a sympathetic look. "I stuck around after you left to see what would happen. As soon as you two were out of the way the truth came out, bit by bit."

I wasn't sure I wanted to hear the rest, but I nodded at Jorge. "Go on."

He shrugged. "At first nobody wanted to talk. But Robert—well, he kind of insisted. So finally the other kids admitted that they spent almost half the time they were supposed to be working doing, um, other things."

"You can say it," I said dully. "They admitted they spent their time goofing off. And that I let them."

Jorge nodded. "Someone even told Robert and Marion about Coco's Construction Concepts." He sighed. "They did not like hearing about that at all. . . ."

The rest of the evening was like more of the same bad dream. Mr. and Mrs. Herrera came home and dragged Veronica off to her own room. They said they were very ashamed of her; they seem to think she was a bad influence on me and the other American visitors. I tried to tell them it was all my fault, but they wouldn't believe me, even after I told them the whole truth about everything that had happened.

I stayed in my room after that, hiding my head under the covers when I heard Kate come in. I didn't want to talk to her. I wasn't sure I would want to talk to anybody ever again. Maybe instead of sending me home, Robert would agree to fly me to Siberia, where I could live out my days all alone, where I couldn't mess up other people's lives or make a big fool of myself.

I couldn't help thinking about how disappointed my parents would be in me. They sent me on this trip because they thought I was a responsible person. I'd really let them down. I'd let down my crew, the Herreras, and all the other nice people of Valle Dulce. I'd let down Robert and Marion and José and the rest of the Rain Forest Friends. And maybe worst of all, I'd let myself down. I'd ignored everything I ever thought was important.

And for what?

# *Eleven*

When I woke up this morning, the first thing I remembered was that we had finished building the recreation center. For a second I felt pretty happy—until I remembered everything that happened after that, and my heart sank like a stone.

When I poked my head out from under the sheet, I saw that Kate was already gone. I didn't blame her. I wouldn't have wanted to stick around and talk to me either.

Somehow I managed to drag myself out of bed and get dressed. I wasn't looking forward to facing the Herreras and the rest of the village. But what choice did I have?

I snuck past the kitchen and headed outside,

hoping to find J.P. before dealing with everybody else. I wanted a chance to explain myself to him—to see if we could make things right again between us. He wasn't at his host family's house, but Andy and Kate were. They told me J.P. had gone into the rain forest right after breakfast to be alone.

Neither of them looked me in the eye while we were talking. They both seemed pretty upset.

"Are you guys mad at me?" I asked, fearing the worst.

They hesitated, looking at each other. Then Kate smiled tentatively.

"Sort of," she admitted in her soft, kind voice. "But we were responsible too. We knew that we weren't following José's instructions. I guess we all just got sort of—swept up in the moment."

I swallowed hard and nodded, grateful that they were being so nice about the whole situation. I liked both of them a lot, and I hated the thought that my carelessness had hurt and embarrassed them.

"Thanks," I said, my voice sounding funny because of the lump in my throat. "I just want you to know I'm—sorry." I choked out the last word and fled.

I headed into the rain forest, listening carefully. J.P. was never very quiet, and I tracked him down soon enough. He was sitting on a log in a small clearing, tossing twigs at a hole in a tree trunk. He looked up quickly when he heard me approaching.

"Oh. It's you." He frowned, then looked away and tossed another twig at the hole. "Shouldn't you be off challenging Tanya to a spelling bee or something?"

"Look, J.P., I know you think I did everything just to win that stupid contest," I said, looking at the ground to avoid his angry gaze. "I wanted you to know that you're wrong. Yes, I did sneak over to get the gas cap so we could start working. But only because I wanted to make sure the villagers got their community center. I'm not ashamed of that. And the reason I cut all those corners after that *wasn't* to beat Tanya."

I paused and took a deep, shaky breath, feeling the tears gathering somewhere just behind my eyes. I knew I had to hurry up and get out what I had to say because I was going to start crying any second.

I gulped and looked him straight in the eye for the first time. "It had nothing to do with Tanya at all. The only reason I did it was to have time to be with you. To have time to play and have fun. I never cared about winning."

He looked a little confused. "Really?" he said. "You did all that for me?"

I nodded and wiped my eyes. "I didn't think you'd like me if I wanted us to work all the time." Then I realized that wasn't quite fair. "Actually," I corrected quickly, "*I* didn't want to work all the time when you were around. I wanted to hang out with you instead."

J.P. dropped the twigs he was holding and leaned back, looking uncertain. There was a moment of silence.

"Anyway," I said at last, "I'll probably be sent home today."

I felt a pang, thinking about that. I couldn't imagine what Mom and Dad would say when they found out. At least I knew that Jessica wouldn't judge me too harshly. Actually, she would probably be proud of me. She'd probably think we were becoming more alike as we got older, and for a while there I would have thought she was right. Now I wasn't so sure. I don't think Jessica has ever felt as guilty about anything in her entire life as I did about the mistakes I'd made on this trip.

Meanwhile J.P. was looking upset at my words. "They can't send you home now." He stood up and hurried over to me. "If they do, I'll go home too!"

"No, you can't, J.P." I grabbed his hands. "Please stay. You have to make sure that Veronica doesn't get in too much trouble. It's all my fault, but her parents don't understand that. You have to help her."

J.P. bit his lip, then he nodded and squeezed my hands. "OK," he said, his face more serious than I had ever seen it. "I guess we owe Veronica something. Both of us."

We didn't talk much after that. He hugged me awkwardly, and then we sat on the log for a while, each of us busy with our own thoughts. Finally I realized that I couldn't stay out here any longer. I had to go back and find out whether I was staying or being sent home in disgrace.

"I've got to go," I said, trying to sound braver than I felt.

J.P. just nodded. "Good luck," he said softly.

I reluctantly went back to the Herreras' house, planning to try one more time to convince Veronica's parents not to punish her for what I had done. When I walked into the kitchen, I found Robert and Marion sitting at the table, waiting for me.

"Hello, Elizabeth," Marion said when I came in. Her normally happy face looked somber. "Sit down, please. We need to talk."

I gulped. So this was it. "Go ahead," I said in a tiny voice, sinking into a chair. My hands were shaking, and my stomach was winding itself in knots. "I'm listening."

Marion and Robert exchanged a glance, then Marion spoke again. "I won't lie to you, Elizabeth. After what happened yesterday, Robert and I discussed sending you home to California today."

"That's right." Robert tapped his long, skinny fingers on the table. "But then we realized that by the time we arranged for a bus to take you back to the city and booked a flight, it would be almost time for you to leave anyway. Besides, one of us would have to escort you to the capital, and we can't really afford that."

Marion smiled for the first time since entering. "True," she said. "But we also realized that you're still pretty young and that you're usually a responsible girl."

What were they saying? I started to hope in spite of myself.

"That's why we've decided to give you a second chance," she said. "An opportunity to help fix your mistakes. We suspected you would welcome that opportunity."

"Although all we really care about is getting the community center built. Built *right*," Robert put in.

Marion ignored him and went on. "This time we're asking José to stay on full-time to supervise. He'll be in charge. But you and your crew will have a chance to repair and rebuild the community center building—if you think you're up to it."

I could hardly believe my ears. They were giving me a second chance? It was more than I deserved. But I wasn't going to tell *them* that. "Definitely!" I exclaimed. "We'll do a fantastic job this time. You'll see!"

Marion smiled at my excitement. "Good," she said, reaching out and patting me on the arm. "I hope you will."

They left to spread the word to the other volunteers, and I just sat there for a few minutes, thinking about how lucky I was. Kate came in a few minutes later, all smiles. She had just heard the news and was just as happy as I was about it. She even hugged me and said she wasn't mad at all anymore.

"Honestly, Elizabeth, this trip has been one of the greatest experiences of my life," she explained. "Andy and I realized that—in a way—we should be thanking you for all the fun we've had. Even if we do have to make up for it now in order to get the community center built."

I was so grateful for her nice words that I couldn't speak for a moment. So I just hugged her again.

We started our repair job right away. At first José frowned every time he glanced at me, but once he saw I was serious about working hard, he eased up a little.

Veronica spent the whole day working steadily along with the rest of us. So did Jorge. They didn't even go home for lunch. They said they wanted to eat with us so they didn't miss a minute of work. In Veronica's case, I suspected she was also avoiding her angry parents.

I didn't blame her. And I didn't forget for one moment that it was all my fault.

MONDAY, *9:05* P.M.

Kate and I are so totally wiped out from work today that we came in to bed right after dinner. Kate is already asleep. But even though my body is tired, my mind is still wide awake.

We're making progress on the community center. José looked over all our work at the end of the day—and actually smiled! I'm starting to think we might really get it finished in time. I'm keeping my fingers crossed!

Veronica is still working like a dog. I think her parents are finally starting to believe she isn't responsible for what happened. Mr. Herrera talked to me about it after breakfast this morning. He said Veronica had always been kind of excitable and flaky, so at first he and her mother were ready to blame her for this mess. But when they thought about it, they realized she had actually been acting more responsible and mature lately than usual. Mr. Herrera even said he still thought I was a good influence on her! Can you believe that? It made me feel kind of good on the one hand but kind of sad on the other because I know I haven't been nearly as good a role model for her as I could have been. But I'm doing my best to make up for that now.

*TUESDAY, 10:00 P.M.*

Even after a really hard day of work, there still seems to be so much more to do before the community center is finished. And no wonder— we were supposed to have five weeks to build this place, and now we're trying to rebuild it in less than a week. I guess all we can do is try our best. At least the foundation is solid.

J.P. and I haven't had much time to be together except at lunch. I miss having fun and hanging, but not as much as I thought I would. It's kind of a relief in a way to be throwing myself into all this hard work. It's a different kind of fun—it's rewarding.

José stood up while we were eating lunch today and told us he was really pleased with our progress. He thinks if we push ourselves as hard as we can for the next day and a half, we can finish the repairs by the end of the day on Friday.

I sure hope he's right. We have to leave the village early Saturday morning to get back to the airport in time for our flight home.

Things at the Herrera house are almost back to normal now. Veronica's parents decided not to punish her when they saw how hard she was working to help make things right. They're proud of her, and I am too. She's a "majorly awesome" friend, and I'll miss her when I go home.

I'll miss this place too. I've really gotten used to falling asleep at night to the sounds of the birds and other creatures of the rain forest. Sweet Valley will seem awfully quiet in comparison!

# *Twelve*

◇

Up until the final hour I was sure we were going to have to leave the community center unfinished. J.P. and Kate were up on the roof nailing on the last few shingles just as the sun dipped down behind the horizon. The rest of us had just finished our final jobs too. José was so happy, he actually hugged Veronica before he realized what he was doing.

But he realized it soon enough and started blushing furiously. "I'd better go call Marion and Robert," he muttered, hurrying off.

The rest of us just stood there for a minute after he left, staring at the rebuilt community center. "I can't believe it's done," I said after a moment. It still hadn't quite sunk in.

"I know," J.P. agreed. "It seems like there should be a thunderclap or something. You know, so we know we really did it."

"No, that's OK," I said quickly, shuddering as I pictured a sudden flash of lightning setting the building on fire. "Just having it finished is enough for me."

Kate smiled. "Still, maybe J.P. is right. Maybe we should have some kind of, you know, house-warming."

"Don't you mean community-center-warming?" J.P. quipped.

But Sumi was nodding. "We *should* do something to celebrate."

"Like what?" Ricky said. "I don't have the energy for another party!" He pretended to collapse on the building's front steps.

I knew what he meant. I was exhausted. But it still seemed as though we should mark the occasion somehow.

"I know!" Veronica said. "Wait here." She raced away before we could question her. She was back five minutes later, holding something. She held it up and winked at me. "Should we try again, *macha?*"

I recognized the ill-fated movie poster. "But how—"

Jorge grinned proudly. "I rescued it from the rubble," he explained. "It wasn't even wrinkled! Well, not much anyway."

This time we all went inside to hang the poster. And this time the walls held as Veronica and I tacked it up.

When we were finished, Veronica and I stepped back to stand with our friends. "It looks *perfecto*," I said.

"*Sí*," Veronica agreed. "Totally awesome!"

"A toast," Mr. Herrera said a little later, holding up his glass. "To our American friends, Elizabeth and Kate!"

Everyone cheered as Kate and I blushed. We were crowded around the dining table with the entire Herrera family, enjoying our last dinner in Costa Rica.

"Thanks," Kate said. "And thanks for letting us stay here."

"There is no need for thanks, *gata*," Mrs. Herrera told her with a smile. "You and Elizabeth are part of our family now. You are always welcome."

"Really?" I blurted it out without thinking. I couldn't help it. I was surprised that Mrs. Herrera would say such a thing—about me, that is, not Kate—after all the trouble I'd caused.

Mrs. Herrera chuckled. "Of course, *macha*," she chided me gently. "We will always consider you part of our family. You have brought our home so much laughter, happiness, and love."

"Totally!" Veronica put in, which made everyone laugh.

"*Sí*, Elizabeth," Jorge said, helping himself to another piece of bread. "And even though Robert and Marion took back that plaque, I think you are an 'outstanding volunteer.'"

"I agree," Mr. Herrera said. "And more important, you're an outstanding person. Both of you," he added, including Kate in his smile.

I was so touched that I was afraid I might start to cry. But at that moment little Eugenia jumped up from her seat. "'Lizabeta! Kate!" she cried. "No go home! You stay!"

"Stay! Stay!" little Ricardo added, pounding on the table with his soupspoon.

That made everyone laugh again, including me. I glanced around at the happy faces of my host family, and for a second I wished that I really could stay. But I knew that even when I was back home in Sweet Valley, I would always remember their kindness.

We sat around the table for a long time, talking and laughing. But finally I excused myself. I had arranged to meet J.P. in the banana grove after dinner. It was time for us to say good-bye. I knew we would see each other tomorrow—after all, we would be on the same plane. But tomorrow was sure to be busy, and rushed, and full of other people. Tonight it would just be us.

He was already waiting for me when I reached the meeting spot. We started walking toward our usual path into the rain forest. We didn't say much at first, just held hands and walked.

Once we were out of sight of the houses, we stopped. He turned to look at me. "You're really great, Elizabeth," he said softly. "I've never met anyone like you."

"You're great too," I replied. I wasn't sure what else to say. Suddenly I had no idea what to say to this guy I'd shared so much with this summer.

So instead of talking, I decided to act. I leaned over and kissed him.

He kissed me back. The kiss was really nice, but this time it had a different sort of mood to it. Does that sound weird? Can a kiss have a mood? Anyway, what I mean is, I think we could both sort of tell that this was some kind of ending.

A week or two ago that would have made me really sad. I hadn't thought I would want my time with J.P. to end. But now I wasn't so sure. Maybe being with him had been the kind of thing that wasn't meant to last too long. I don't know. But I noticed he hadn't said anything about getting together after we got back home, even though we only lived a few miles apart. And I didn't quite feel like saying it either.

Eventually the kiss just sort of drifted off, and we moved apart. J.P. looked down at his feet. "So I guess this is it, huh, Bob?"

"Something like that," I agreed, smiling at the goofy nickname in spite of myself. "School will be starting pretty soon."

That reminded me of the gossip back home in Sweet Valley. I wondered if everybody knew what was happening with the schools yet. Maybe I would find out tomorrow. Maybe not.

Either way, I realized as J.P. and I wandered back toward the village, I would deal with it. My trip to Costa Rica had been really educational, though not in the ways I had expected. I found out a lot about myself—maybe more than I really wanted to know. But I guess I'm glad I did. Because even if my attitude didn't change completely, even if I'm not ready to blow off all my responsibilities and concentrate on fun (like a certain twin of mine), I think I have changed at least a little.

I hope I won't ever totally toss my responsibilities out the window again like I did for a few weeks there. That was way too extreme. Then again, maybe the way I always was before this trip was another kind of extreme. Maybe I've been *too* serious and responsible up until now.

Is it possible to find a way to live in between those two extremes? I don't know, but I'm going to try. I'm still going to take school and other things seriously, but I also want to make some real time for fun, maybe even for romance. Who knows? In any case, I expect that will make eighth grade a whole lot more interesting—no matter what happens.

I just hope the people back home can handle my cool new attitude!

*What does the eighth grade have in store for Elizabeth? Find out in the brand-new series, **Sweet Valley Jr. High!***

Bantam Books in the SWEET VALLEY TWINS series.
Ask your bookseller for the books you have missed.

## Sweet Valley Twins Super Editions

## Sweet Valley Twins Super Chiller Editions

## Sweet Valley Twins Magna Editions